Praise for

dark waters

"The fast-paced plot, with its element of the supernatural, explores moral and ethical issues, providing conflict and depth to the story's mystery and adventure."
—*Kirkus Reviews*

"A realistic page-turner . . . A good solid read that explores some darker themes, yet has an uplifting ending."   —*School Library Journal*

"A fast-moving, pithily written moral tale."
—*Bulletin of the Center for Children's Books*

"MacPhail's book neither trivializes nor romanticizes the decisions Col makes. The issues Col faces will strike a chord with adolescents who struggle with similar ethical choices."
—*SIGNAL Journal*

"A spooky mystery."   —*The Seattle Times*

CATHERINE MACPHAIL

is the author of several novels for teens, including *Missing* and the upcoming *Underworld*. She lives with her family in Scotland.

dark waters

CATHERINE MACPHAIL

BLOOMSBURY

Thanks to Stewart S.,
a real-life hero

Published by Bloomsbury Publishing, New York and London
Distributed to the trade by Holtzbrinck Publishers

Library of Congress Cataloging-in-Publication Data
MacPhail, Catherine.
Dark waters / Catherine Macphail.
p. cm.
Summary: Col McCann becomes a local hero when he saves a boy from drowning
but when his older brother is suspected of a serious crime, Col must decide if he should
be loyal to his family or tell the truth about what he saw while under water.
ISBN-10: 1-58234-846-4 (hardcover)
ISBN-13: 978-1-58234-846-9 (hardcover)
ISBN-10: 1-58234-986-X (paperback)
ISBN-13: 978-1-58234-986-2 (paperback)
[1. Heros—Fiction. 2. Brothers—Fiction. 3. Loyalty—Fiction. 4. Ghosts—Fiction. 5. Conduct of
life—Fiction. 6. Scotland—Fiction.] I. Title.
PZ7.M2426 Dar 2003   [Fic]—dc21   2002028296

Printed in the U.S.A.
1 3 5 7 9 10 8 6 4 2

Bloomsbury Publishing, Children's Books, U.S.A
175 Fifth Avenue, New York, NY 10010

All papers used by Bloomsbury Publishing are natural, recyclable products
made from wood grown in well-managed forests. The manufacturing processes
conform to the environmental regulations of the country of origin.

For Archie

CHAPTER ONE

Was his mother going to be mad, or what! He'd forgotten to tape her favourite soap. Again. Col flopped back on the sofa, not too worried. Och well, the daft old bat shouldn't trust him to remember things like that. Not when there was football on the other side. Mind you, he thought, he'd better never call her a daft old bat to her face. His mam thought she was quite a foxy lady with her blonde hair and her trim figure, and she was still in her forties . . . just.

'If you were that foxy,' he would tell her, 'you'd be out getting another man, not spending all your nights at bingo.'

And she would always reply, 'I've had one man. The best. Don't want another. The only man I'm interested in now is the one who calls out the numbers at the bingo.'

That *one* man had been his dad, the original McCann. Col could hardly remember him. He was only six when his father was killed – driving a getaway car in a robbery, crashing it during the police chase. What Col could remember was a big, broad bull of a man who scared everyone in the town, except Col. He had always seemed to make Col laugh.

Maybe, Col thought hopefully, his mam would win at bingo tonight. Then her soap would be forgotten. And he wouldn't be in her bad books.

The sky outside suddenly lit up and sheets of icy rain crashed against the window. 'I hope she gets a taxi home,' he thought. 'Or a lift.' He didn't like the idea of his mother walking home, or even waiting for a bus on a night like this.

Not that she'd be in any real danger, he considered. She was a McCann, and no one in this town would dare touch her. They'd know what to expect in return. His brother Mungo would see to them.

But still, when Col was older the first thing he was going to do was buy a car, then he'd take his mam to bingo and pick her up again.

He couldn't wait till he was old enough to have a car. He could already drive. Mungo had taught him, letting him race about in one of his dodgy cars on the old derelict industrial estate nearby. Revving up the engine, screeching round corners. Col loved it. It made him feel alive.

'You can drive my getaway car any day,' Mungo would say.

But never when Mam could hear him. She knew Mungo saw his dad as some kind of hero and was following in his footsteps. She was terrified Col would end up the same way.

A crack of thunder right above the house made him jump. He wished his brother would come home, too. He'd hoped Mungo would have stayed in tonight so they could have watched the football together.

'Not the night, wee man, there's something that's got to be handled.' And he had tapped his nose in that secret way he did when what was to be handled was too secret even for Col.

Trouble. Mungo was either going to cause it, or be in it.

One day, Col would be right there with his brother. Knowing all there was to know. He'd be with Mungo. Just like Mungo. A McCann. Putting the fear of death into people. Col couldn't wait.

Right at that second, Mungo burst in through the

front door bringing the storm with him. Col jumped to his feet.

'Mungo! What's wrong?'

His brother looked scared, almost panic-stricken. He was soaked through, covered in mud, and his face was bleeding and swollen.

'You been in a fight?'

Stupid question. Of course he had.

Mungo slammed the door hard behind him. 'Cops are after me, Col.' He glanced towards the street as if he could almost see them. 'They'll be here any minute.'

And already, in the distance, Col could hear the faint sound of a siren wailing closer.

'Where can I hide, Col?'

Col was thinking fast. 'You don't need somewhere to hide, bruv. You need an alibi.'

Mungo managed a swollen, lopsided smile. 'Aye, but I can't exactly say I've been sitting by the fire all night looking like this, can I?'

The police car was turning into their street, homing in on his brother.

Suddenly, Col grabbed Mungo by the shoulders. 'Come on!' he shouted, and began to drag him towards the back door.

'What's your game?'

Col pulled harder. 'I'm giving you an alibi.'

He yanked open the back door and the storm raged into the kitchen. With a violent push Col threw Mungo out into the back garden. Mungo landed with a splash and a howl of anger on the sodden, muddy grass.

'What the—' he started to yell angrily, but before he could get to his feet Col threw himself on top of him, sending him even deeper into the mud.

He grabbed Mungo by the jacket. 'We've been in the house all night. Just you and me. Right? We've argued about the game. Our team lost 2–1. They were rubbish. But you don't think so. You think they were robbed. We don't fight in the house, Mam won't allow it, so . . . here we are . . .'

All the time he was speaking Col was pulling Mungo round so they were rolling together on the long wet grass while the rain belted down on them.

Mungo yelled with delight, grabbed a handful of mud and rubbed it over Col's head. 'You're brilliant, Col.' Now, he was on top of Col, pulling at his shirt, grinding his face into the mud.

They both stopped for a second as the front door was pounded. Another flash of lightning lit up Mungo's face, eerie in the strange, white light.

'They're here,' Mungo said, breathlessly.

'You've got to punch me, Mungo. Make it look real. Punch me hard.'

Mungo shook his head. 'Naw, no' you, Col. I couldn't hit my brother.'

The pounding grew fiercer.

'You've not got a choice,' he said, closing his eyes as his brother raised his fist. Mungo, the hardest man in the town, renowned for his fighting skills yet he'd never laid a finger on Col.

Mungo closed his eyes too. 'Sorry, bruv.'

The blow took Col by surprise. He felt as if he'd been hit by a sledgehammer. He gasped. His nose immediately began to bleed and when he opened his eyes he saw strange, starlike dots in front of him and two visions of Mungo not quite merging into one.

Mungo hauled him to his feet. 'Come on. We'd better answer that door before they break it down.'

Col staggered upright. He thought he was going to be sick. It was the blood. He could taste it.

They had only just made it back into the kitchen when the front door flew open and his mother hurried in with two policemen looming behind her. A sudden gust rushed through the house, sending curtains flying and dishes rattling, before the back door suddenly hurled itself shut.

'What is going on here!' Grace McCann shouted angrily. 'I come back to find two polis nearly breakin' my house down. What is going on!'

She threw her bag on the kitchen table and ran to Col. She grabbed him just in time as his knees buckled under him. She lowered him gently on to the chair and glared at her elder son. 'What have you done?'

'He was slaggin' off our team. Taught him a lesson.'

Col tried to talk through a mouthful of blood. 'They were rubbish. I taught *you* the lesson.'

That made their mother even madder. 'I can't believe you two were fighting over a daft game of football.'

'No. Neither can we.' The taller of the two policemen stared straight at Mungo. 'You're trying to tell us you've been in all night? That your wee brother did that?' He pointed to Mungo's swollen face, his cut lip.

Mungo grinned. 'Sure did. He's a great wee fighter. But then, he's a McCann.'

Their mother jumped to her son's defence. 'Right. What's Mungo getting the blame for now?'

The other policeman's voice was calm. 'Been a lot of

trouble on the edge of the town tonight. Some kind of battle.'

'Oh, of course, and if there's some kind of battle Mungo McCann must be to blame.'

'He was seen running away, Mrs McCann.'

Grace McCann put her hands on her hips defiantly. 'Who saw him? You?'

His pause told her the answer. 'No. Not you! Someone else saw him . . . or says they did. When in doubt blame a McCann. I'll go and see our lawyer the morrow.'

The big policeman nodded. 'You probably will, Mrs McCann. You know so much more about the law than we do.'

'Just as well,' she snapped. 'Now, as you can see my two boys have been in all night. So you go and find somebody else to harass.'

'We're going. I dare say we'll be back. We usually are.' His gaze at Mungo was full of contempt.

Mungo drew himself up arrogantly and stared right back at him.

'How could you do that to your own brother?' the policeman said bitterly. 'He's only a boy. You really are a McCann, aren't you?'

He turned to leave and as he did so Mungo was almost after him. His body was ready to spring. Col held him back, shook his head. Mungo relaxed but he was angry.

'I shouldn't have hit you, Col,' he said as soon as the door had closed behind the police.

'No, indeed you shouldn't!' Their mam exploded now with rage. 'I will not have you turning on your brother, for any reason. Family's the most important thing in the world. You never turn against your family. Do you hear me, Mungo?'

Mungo shrank back when his mother railed at him. 'But you don't understand, Mam—'

She didn't let him finish. 'I understand enough to know you don't ever turn on your brother.'

Mungo stepped back, bent his head, and said nothing more. Neither did Col. They both knew it was better to keep quiet when Grace McCann lost her temper. She was a tiger when she got started. And, anyway, the less their mother knew about this the better.

'I'm going to run you a bath, Col. And as for you . . .' She glared at her elder son. 'I'll have more to say to you later.'

Col limped up the stairs behind his mother. The

fight, the night, had taken more out of him than he'd thought.

'Col,' Mungo called up to him as he was halfway up the stairs. 'I'll make this up to you, bruv. I'll get you a really special present.'

Col looked down at his brother. Mungo was still muddy and bleeding but even now there was a cockiness about him that scared people, but attracted them too. Mungo was everything Col ever wanted to be. Feared and admired and despised. He was the best big brother anyone could ever have.

He'd never do anything to hurt him.

He'd die before he'd ever turn against him.

CHAPTER TWO

'That's some keeker you've got, McCann.'

Thelma Blaikie shouted to him across the playground. Her spiky hair was as black as his eye had become over the weekend. She sauntered over to him, chewing her gum, trying to look cool.

She fancied herself as his girlfriend. She wished. Thelma Blaikie was as hard as nails, always in trouble at school – when she was there. She seemed to think that mapped her out as a suitable bird for a McCann. No way. Though, even Col could see she had the potential to be a stunner . . . in spite of the Gothic white face and the black eyes. But as soon as Blaikie opened her mouth she spoiled everything. Blaikie's voice could grate cheese. She was too loud, too brash, always it seemed to Col trying to impress him.

Like now. She stopped in front of him and blew a

bubble right in his face. He was tempted to flatten it all over her ghost-white cheeks.

It burst with a bang and she sucked it back into her mouth. She laughed. 'Big fight at the weekend? Heard there was trouble up your way.'

Col shrugged. 'Nothing to do with us. Me and Mungo were in all night. This . . .' he pointed to his eye, 'was an accident.'

'Some accident. Want me to kiss it better?'

Col curled his lip in disgust. 'I'd rather be eaten by tarantulas.' He walked away from her while she stood watching him, still trying to look cool.

His mate, Denny, ran up behind him. 'You're well in there, Col.' As Col turned to face him, Denny's eyes lit up. 'Wow! What bus hit you?'

He told Denny the same story he told Blaikie. Mates they might have been. Bosom buddies they were not. The lie would be all he would ever tell anyone. The truth would be between him and his brother.

Every teacher that morning asked him the same question, and was given the same answer.

Except for Mrs Holden, the Maths teacher. She and Col had long ago decided they didn't like each other. She had also taught Mungo, remembered him from his time at the school. Remembered the trouble he had caused her, and every other teacher. She'd expected the same trouble from the younger McCann, and Col hadn't disappointed her. When he paid no attention in class, he made sure no one else did either.

She didn't ask what had happened to him. Not out loud. But her eyebrow lifted, ever so slightly, when he strolled in late to her class.

'It's OK, Mrs Holden,' Col explained. 'I was having an intellectual discussion about algebra, and the other guy lost his temper. See, these mathematicians . . . they cannae take a joke.'

Denny laughed. Most of the class did, too. Only Mrs Holden's face remained stony.

'It would be nice to know you could be passionate about something, Col,' was all she said.

If only she knew the truth, Col thought, as he slid down in his seat. Would she ever have done what he did for his brother? Somehow, he didn't think so. Part of him wanted to tell her, to shout it to the world. But no, it had to be a secret, a McCann secret, and that's how it would stay.

The cold wet weather turned to ice and the hilly town

became treacherous. The cold seemed to seep into the bones and the school's central heating hardly took the chill off the air. One afternoon just a few days later, Col decided not to go back after lunch at the chippie. He wanted to breathe in the ice-cold air, and if he was going to be cold, he'd rather be cold outside than in. If anything, his face looked worse, the bruise turning blue then green, and the endless questions about it were beginning to annoy him. He wandered aimlessly up through the town, over the hills, past the local prison and the hospital. Someone waved from a prison window and Col waved back. He wondered what it would be like to be locked up, to have that door slam shut, and locked behind you – to know you weren't free to leave whenever you wanted. He'd hate it. Mungo had been locked up. More than once, on remand. And he had hated it. He prided himself on the fact they had never been able to make any charge stick.

'I'm too smart for them, son,' he would tell Col.

Col walked on. The town was well behind him now. He loved how it never took long to leave civilisation behind him here. One minute he would be right in the middle of the bustle, the noise – squabbling children, angry mothers, traffic – and the next he would be deep in the calm of the hills and the bracken and the loch. He loved coming here. He could think, and be quiet and alone.

It was hardly a loch. Not exactly your Loch Lomond, more a very large pond with swans and ducks; but it was peaceful, especially now with a misty, icy fog descending on the January afternoon.

Col squatted on the grass. He was already freezing. He was daft. Mungo, if he knew he had come here, would think he was crazy. He could be sitting by the fire right now, pretending to his mother that his belly ached. He could be home, getting spoiled. Hot broth, chips, his favourite comics.

He'd go in a minute, he decided. And yet, it was so peaceful here on this icy, dark afternoon.

There was a sudden squawk as a couple of ducks slid along the ice. Col laughed. They seemed to be arguing with each other. Man and wife, he imagined, blaming each other for something. He leaned forward to watch their progress and for the first time he noticed another solitary figure at the edge of the loch. A boy, much younger than Col, ten maybe, testing the ice with the heel of his shoe. He was wearing a maroon blazer. St Roch's. Posh, fee-paying school nearby. Col watched him as he took one tentative step on to the loch. There were signs everywhere warning of thin ice. The boy took no notice, but then ten-year-old boys never did. He took a few steps further, more confident as he realised that the ice was holding.

Col could almost hear him think, 'Thin Ice? Who are they trying to kid?' Col had done it himself many times.

The boy was beginning to get cocky. He did a little dance on the ice, then, embarrassed, looked all around him quickly to make sure no one was there to see him. Col darted back behind the bushes, hung with frost. But only for a moment.

The boy, now convinced he was alone, let out a yell of delight and went sliding almost to the middle of the loch. The two ducks squawked in annoyance and slid out of his way.

The ice in the middle held him too. Col could see his confidence growing. To make sure, the boy jumped once, twice, three times.

Col was beginning to think this wee boy was one sandwich short of a picnic. The ice in the middle of the loch probably wasn't as thick as this boy was.

The boy looked all around him, thinking. Then he turned and began skating back to the edge. Col was almost relieved. This wee fool had taken enough chances. His eyes followed the boy back to the bank, watched with interest as he picked up his rucksack and took something out and stuffed it into his mouth. By the way he began to chew it had to be a caramel. The boy dropped the rucksack and turned his gaze towards the loch. Still deep in thought. There was a determination in his step as he headed back.

What on earth was this idiot about to do now?

Col didn't have to wait long to find out.

The boy lifted a boulder from the ground. It was almost as big as he was. Still chewing, he hoisted it up in his arms and struggled back on to the ice.

'I don't believe this!' Col muttered softly.

The boy staggered into the middle of the ice again. It was growing darker by the minute and the icy fog was descending fast. He lifted the boulder as high as he was able and, suddenly, he hurled it down on the ice.

Col let out a low whistle. Crazy! he thought.

But it seemed to be all the proof the boy needed. He began to jump wildly up and down on the ice, cheering. As if he and the ice were in competition against each other, and he had won.

The boy was mad.

Col's eyes were drawn back to the rucksack, lying half open, so close by.

He wondered if there were any more caramels in it. If there was, perhaps there'd be something more than caramels. Money.

St Roch's. Fee-paying school.

Wee snotrag would be bound to have money. Mummy and Daddy probably gave him lots of dosh.

Col edged towards the rucksack. He was hidden by the bracken and the bushes. No one else was here. No one but him and this boy.

He'd lifted the boulder again. Not content, wanting to test it one more time. He never even glanced Col's way.

Col moved silently. The rucksack lay open. Col could see books and jotters. He could even make out the tube of sweets.

The sudden crash of the boulder against the ice made him jump. He shot a glance across the loch, but the boy was only interested in the ice and the boulder. He was whooping like a Comanche brave on the warpath.

Col reached the rucksack, crouched down lower and began to finger through the books and jotters. Here, a bookmark; there, yuck, a sticky caramel half chewed. But then!

What was this? A crisp, ten-pound note.

Col leaned forward, ready to slip it out. Wee fool deserved all he got anyway.

Right then there was a sudden ominous crack. A yell. A panicked scream. Col looked up.

The boy was dancing on the ice again.

No. This time he wasn't dancing. He was trying to balance. The ice beneath him was cracking. The boy tried to jump clear, but he landed badly and broke more ice.

Col saw the panic on the boy's face as his arms flailed wildly and his feet jumped and slid about in a grotesque dance.

Mesmerised, unable to move, Col watched. The boy still hadn't seen him, couldn't see anything beyond his own peril. He wasn't even screaming or shouting. He was trying to jump clear but, with every movement, the ice moved, cracked, broke beneath him.

'It's your own fault!' Col wanted to yell. Stupid boy had brought it on himself, hadn't he?

The ice on which the boy had been standing suddenly toppled almost upright, and the panic-stricken boy began to slip into the icy waters of the loch.

Col stood up, paralysed, unable to move. Nothing to

do with him anyway, he kept telling himself. Couldn't the boy read? The notices everywhere. BEWARE. THIN ICE. His own fault.

The boy was yelling at the top of his voice.

'Mum! Mum! Help me! Please! Mum!'

He was clawing at the ice, trying to pull himself up. His fingers clutched and scraped but couldn't get a grip.

Inside, Col was screaming too. 'Your own fault! You deserve it! Who cares? I don't. I *don't*!'

The boy was sobbing now, and Col tried to blot out his anguished cries.

'Please! Please! Somebody help me!'

Not me. Not me, was all Col could think. Definitely not *me*! In the same instant he was running, pulling off his jacket, running towards the boy in the icy loch – and changing his life for ever.

CHAPTER THREE

The boy saw Col coming, rushing towards him in a
frenzy. His face was white with panic, with cold. He was
breathing hard and fast, still clawing at the ice. Col
skidded towards him, thinking as fast as he could. Trying to forget that now, he too was in the middle of the
loch, with only breaking ice and swirling currents
beneath him. Yet, his brain was clear, cool. He threw
himself flat, and swung his jacket towards the boy.

'Grab this!' he snapped. Not angrily. He wasn't angry.
He was so calm now it almost scared him. But he had to
calm the boy in the loch. 'Grab this!' he said again. An
order.

The boy's hands were shaking, so cold his fingers
would hardly close, but still he reached out for Col's
jacket. Without the support of the ice he lost his hold
for a second and panic gripped him as the water, the

clinging reeds, began to pull him down. Col edged closer, grabbed the boy's hands just as his face was covered by the freezing water. He hauled him up.

And felt the ice below him crack.

No!

Col swung the jacket again and this time, with Col's support, the boy's grip was firm. Col bellied his way back slowly. 'I'm going to pull. You keep holding tight.' He realised his teeth were chattering.

The boy's only answer was his numbed fingers closing on the jacket. Col edged back cautiously. He could feel the ice move under him.

This time the crack was heard by the boy. His eyes, half shut, snapped open in terror. Terror at the thought of his saviour crashing through the ice, of both of them in the water, drowning, dying. It was too much for him. He began to scream, to thrash about. That was the last thing Col needed.

'Stay calm.' Col was surprised at how soft, how gentle his own voice sounded. If he could keep him calm, keep moving back along the ice, pull the boy at least halfway out of the loch, then maybe . . . just maybe, they might both be all right.

But all the boy could see was death and cold, and the

terror of it overcame him. He started to flail about wildly. He let go of the jacket, grabbed for Col's arms. Missed. Screamed.

He was about to go under again, and Col knew that this time he wouldn't be able to haul him up.

He would have to let him drown. What else was there for him to do?

Yet still he found himself moving forward, grabbing for the boy's arm, his hand, his hair. His almost numb fingers gripped at last the collar of his blazer. The boy was squirming, splashing, screaming. But at last he had him. Col pulled with a strength he never knew he had. With one yank he had him shoulder high out of the loch. He screeched, and grabbed for Col's elbows. Now he was waist high. Col almost had him out of the icy water. One more pull. Just one more—

In that instant the ice cracked again. This time it didn't hold. Col felt his legs being dragged down into the freezing water that burned into his bones. Still he didn't let the boy go. Now he pushed, pushed him up and on to strong thick ice, and as one boy rose out of the water to safety, the other, Col, was sucked under by a swirl of currents that seemed almost alive.

NO!

He sent the boy sliding along the ice. Let him go. Reached out for something to hold on to himself. But he found nothing, only ice that scraped through his fingers.

He wouldn't die this way! No!

He clawed, grappled at the ice, but his fingers, too cold, too numb, found nothing to hold on to. The cold took the breath from him.

He was going under.

The boy struggled to his feet. He was crying, looking around for help. Too young, too scared to know what to do.

This is your fault, Col wanted to scream at him. Yours!

And as the waters closed around his head, he could still see the boy shimmering above him, running towards him. Still screaming.

But Col couldn't hear him now.

He was in a silent, eerie world.

Reeds brushed against his face, clutched at his ankles as if they were pulling him down, welcoming him into their cold watery world.

For ever.

He thought he could see Mungo's angry face through

the ice, angry that he should die this way, trying to save a boy who had it all coming to him.

And his mother too. He was almost sure he could see her standing on the ice with the boy, crying uncontrollably.

But who else would cry for Col McCann?

Nobody.

The ice was closing above him and through the dark waters frightening images floated towards him. Reeds undulated in the current. Then became faces, ghostly, uncanny faces, calling to him silently. This was their world. And soon it would be his. His for ever. Col, with hardly any life behind him, now had none in front of him.

Floating ferns wrapped themselves around him, and something else. Something so close he could almost reach out and touch it. Something he didn't want to face.

Something terrifying was there in the loch with him.

Did Death have a face?

No! No! No!

He wouldn't look at it.

He wouldn't be lost in these dark waters for ever.

He began to struggle wildly again and, suddenly –

where did he get the strength from? – he was surging up and up and up, almost as if he was being pushed. Kicking with frozen legs, with all the determination of someone who just wasn't ready to die.

He broke the surface with a wild cry.

This time he grabbed, kicked, hung on. He was never going under there again.

Never!

And by the time the ambulance arrived Col was unconscious, half dead, lying on the broken ice of the loch.

CHAPTER FOUR

Col opened his eyes slowly. A girl was bending over him, white like an angel, except for her chocolate-brown face.

Where was he? In heaven? Had he died and gone to heaven? He couldn't remember a thing for a moment. Couldn't understand why he was here, or even where he was. He was disorientated, exhausted, still struggling for breath.

'You're awake at last.' The nurse – she was a nurse – smiled widely. Her teeth were the brightest white he had ever seen. Col wanted to smile back, but it was too exhausting. 'You've just missed your mother. She's been here all the time, sitting by your bed. We sent her home for a rest half an hour ago.'

While she spoke she was tucking him in, lifting his wrist, checking his pulse against her watch. *Am I still alive?* he wanted to ask. He tried to speak, but his mouth was so dry the words just wouldn't come. He glanced sideways and realised he was on a drip. He tried to remember how he got here, but his memory, his brain, something, wasn't working.

'Everyone's been praying for you, you know. The whole hospital. The whole town.' She still smiled as she jotted down notes on a clipboard at the foot of his bed.

Praying for me? He thought he'd said it aloud, but he hadn't. His voice just wouldn't come. The nurse came close and touched his shoulder gently. 'You're a hero, Col.' She walked to the door. 'I'll ring your mother, but until she comes back I want you to rest. OK? That's what you need after all you've been through, complete rest.' She closed the door softly behind her, and he was alone.

What he'd *been through*?

What had he been through? He looked around the clean, white hospital room, at the window and the darkening, heavy sky outside. He could see the snow-tipped hills, and the icy January fog descending over the town.

Something stirred in his memory. Something he didn't want to remember.

He was a hero.

Exhaustion was pulling his eyelids shut. He could feel himself drifting away on an ocean with a hot sun beating down on him, gentle waves lapping at his feet. But as he drifted deeper into sleep the water grew colder. And he wasn't on a raft any more, but an ice floe surrounded by icebergs. And the ice floe was tipping and slanting under him. Slipping him under the water into a silent world with reeds and strange underwater creatures tugging at him, dragging him down. He struggled to be awake, to get above the water away from the faces that floated eerily in front of him. Faces he knew. Strange faces he had never seen before, drifting towards him through the waving reeds. Now he remembered! He remembered everything. The boy. The ice. And *Death* – reaching out to get him and him only just escaping.

Aagh! He jumped awake, sweat pouring from him, his breath coming in short desperate gasps.

And he wasn't alone.

A boy was sitting on his bed, staring at him, smiling. Wearing Scotland team pyjamas. He knew his face. Had seen him before wearing a St Roch's uniform.

'Oh good. You're awake.' The boy bounced on the bed enthusiastically. 'I'm not supposed to be in here. I'll get murdered for coming. I had to sneak in. My room's down there.' He pointed somewhere down the corridor. 'The nurse – she's called Cleo by the way – nice, isn't she? Well, she says you weren't to be disturbed, but you had woken up and were going to be fine.' He bounced closer to Col and took a breath. 'We thought you were going to die, Col.'

Col! This wee snotrag was calling him by his first name as if he was his best friend.

'I'm Dominic. Dominic Sampson. The boy whose life you saved!' He said it dramatically and emblazoned an imaginary headline in the air. 'Sounds good doesn't it?' He patted Col's arm. 'You don't say a word. Preserve your strength. I'll do all the talking.'

Somehow Col didn't think that would be a problem for Dominic Sampson.

'My mum and dad are *so* angry with me. You'd think they'd be happy I was still alive, but they just keep going on about staying away from thin ice, etcetera, etcetera . . .' He rolled his eyes.

Col wished he had the strength to punch him. If the boy had stayed away from thin ice, Col wouldn't be here.

'I mean, I was sure I would be OK. I'm a really good swimmer.'

A really good swimmer! Now Col really did feel like punching him. He could hardly swim a stroke.

'But you see, I panicked and you didn't. You were brilliant, Col. Brilliant. You saved my life.'

Saving Dominic's life was something Col was starting

to regret.

Dominic edged closer to him. 'Do you know, some ancient tribes believe that if you save somebody's life that person belongs to you for ever?'

Col felt a surge of panic. Dominic Sampson was already beginning to get on his wick. Dominic suddenly jumped off the bed. He seemed only ever to bounce or jump anywhere. 'You, Col, are my hero. And my life is yours now. You ask anything of me and I'll get it for you.' He slid along the polished floor and pulled the door open. 'It's a myth . . . or do I mean a legend?' He laughed suddenly. 'Or maybe I just made it up.'

Then he was gone.

Col had saved Dominic Sampson's life, and risked his own. Why? What had made him do such a thing? He couldn't find any answer to that.

In the quiet, Col almost drifted back to sleep but he didn't dare. Too afraid of the dark dreams that might come.

Cleo came back in later, checking his drip, as beautiful as before.

'Can't you sleep?'

At last, with a struggle, Col found his voice. 'Dreams. Bad dreams. The water . . . going under. Not being able to get up.'

She stopped her ministrations and sat on the bed.

'It's understandable, Col. You've been through a major trauma. You almost died. You saved a boy's life. It's probably the most dramatic thing that's ever happened to you.'

Col nodded.

'So I suppose your subconscious has got to go over it again and again, just to come to terms with it.'

She rubbed his hand gently. 'I had a baby four months ago. And that was the most traumatic thing that ever happened to me. After the birth, every time I closed my eyes I relived every moment, I couldn't get it out of my mind. But then, it fades. And what you're left with is a beautiful baby, worth it all. It will fade for you too, Col. And what you'll have is the memory of the bravest thing anyone can ever do. Risk their own life to save someone else.'

She looked at him as if she thought he was wonderful.

Had he really done anything so fearless? He didn't remember it like that.

'You're a real-life hero, Col. And I'm very proud to be your nurse.'

When she'd gone, he closed his eyes, wanting desperately to just sleep.

When he did, finally, his sleep was deep and dreamless.

CHAPTER FIVE

'You wee devil!' His mother threw herself at him and hugged him close. Col could feel her tears against his face.

'Mam!' His embarrassed voice was like a croak. He pushed her away and she took a seat beside him, sniffing quietly into a handkerchief.

Mungo was there too. Standing grim-faced at the bottom of the bed.

'Hi, bruv.'

Col smiled at him.

Mungo didn't smile back. 'What the hell were you thinking about?' he snapped at him angrily. 'You could have died! They thought you had died. Do you know what you've put Mam through? And for what! To save a poncy wee snob. You risked your life for that!'

Mam touched his arm. 'Sssh, Mungo. Leave the boy

be, he's been through enough.'

'I know. I was st-stupid.' Col stuttered out the words, hurt at his brother's attitude.

'You don't go near that loch again. Hear me!' Mungo came close to him. Said again, fiercely, 'Hear me! I don't want you anywhere near that loch.'

Col nodded.

'Mungo was worried about you as well, Col,' Mam said softly.

Of course he was, Col thought. But why so angry? The answer, it seemed, came with Mungo's next words. 'Do you think these people would have done the same for you?'

Cleo came in then, still smiling. 'Feel better now your mum's here, Col?'

Mam clutched at his hand. 'A boy always needs his mother.'

Cleo came and fussed around him. 'Just got to give you your medicine. Won't be a minute.'

She wasn't. She even made the medicine taste good. Col smiled. Before she left she offered his mother a cup of tea. His mother nodded.

Nurse Cleo turned to Mungo then. 'And what about you, Mr McCann? Tea for you as well?'

'That would be lovely, darlin'.' He winked at her. 'Unless you've got anything stronger.'

When she'd gone Mungo turned to Col. 'Got to be nice to them sometimes, eh? At least they make good nurses.'

Col was suddenly embarrassed by his brother. He hoped he would never talk like that in front of Cleo. He'd never want her to be hurt.

Yet, he was surprised at himself too. Not too long ago he would have said exactly the same thing.

He was glad it wasn't Cleo who brought in the tea. Instead, it was a nursing assistant. A man he'd never seen before.

In his wake, came more visitors. The Sampson family.

Dominic burst into the room with an excited shout of welcome. 'Col, I've brought my mum and dad. They've been dying to meet you.'

He was dragging in a woman, her strawberry-blonde hair cut into a soft bob. She was wearing a rich-looking camel-hair coat. Close behind her was Dominic's father. He was well dressed too. Dark-blue overcoat, long scarf, his hair tinged with grey. Col thought he looked a bit like Sean Connery.

Dominic dived on to the bed. 'This is Col,' he said

proudly, as if Col was an exhibit in a museum. Col noticed that Mungo had taken a step back, was almost ignoring them. And because of that Mam kept her eyes glued to the floor.

Mrs Sampson stepped towards him. A faint waft of flowery perfume drifted about her. 'I don't know how to thank you, Col. If it hadn't been for you we would have lost the most precious thing we have.'

Dominic bounced again. 'That's me.'

'Because of your stupidity, Dominic, Col might not be alive. Do you realise that?' His mother's angry tone made Dominic's smile disappear. 'Because you never obey rules, because you were stupid enough to go out on to that ice an innocent boy could have died.' She looked now directly at Mam. Mam had no choice but to look up at her. 'I think you must resent us, Mrs McCann. I know how I'd feel.'

Mam nodded. 'I'm glad you realise that, Mrs Sampson. If I'd lost my boy . . .' She let the words trail off, and tightened her grip on Col's hand.

'I know. I know. I'm sorry we're interrupting your visit. But I . . . we wanted to come in and thank you personally.'

For the first time Mr Sampson spoke. 'If there's

anything you need, Col. Just let us know.'

Mungo butted in. 'If Col needs anything, I can supply it.'

Mr Sampson looked at Mungo, and Col could see that Dominic's dad, his whole family, knew all about the McCanns and their reputation – especially Mungo's.

'Of course. I'm sorry.' Mr Sampson's voice was soft when he answered. 'But we are so grateful, we feel there must be something we could do to thank Col.'

There was an awkward silence until Mrs Sampson took Dominic by the hand and pulled him off the bed. 'I think we should leave Col with his family now.'

'Can't I stay?' Dominic's eyes pleaded with Col, but his mother was having none of it.

'No, you cannot. I think you've given Col quite enough trouble.'

As Dominic was dragged out he called back, 'I'll come in and see you later. OK?' He didn't wait for an answer. He seemed sure this was something Col would look forward to. 'I'm only down the corridor if you need me.'

Mr Sampson backed out behind him. 'I'm afraid he means it, Col. But if he's being any bother, just let me know.'

'They seem like a nice family,' Mam said when they'd gone.

'I'm never going to get rid of that Dominic. He thinks I'm a hero.'

Col wanted Mungo to smile at him. Just once. But he didn't. Instead, he growled. 'Do you know this has been a front-page story for the past two days? We've had reporters at the house and everything. I don't like it, Col.'

Mungo didn't like any kind of publicity. Although up to now the only kind he'd had was bad publicity – arrest, breach of the peace, housebreaking, not-proven verdicts from local juries too scared to convict him.

'It's a nine-day wonder, Mungo,' Mam said. 'It was a brave thing you did, Col.' But she said it softly almost as if she didn't want Mungo to hear.

It was a difficult visit and Col was almost glad to see them go.

But he wasn't alone for long.

Col had settled down in the bed, sleep beginning to steal over him, when he had a feeling that someone was in the room with him. He opened his eyes, slowly.

A young man, maybe the same age as Mungo, stood beside the bed. He looked dirty, unshaven; as if he hadn't washed for a while. His dark hair was long and unkempt.

Col sat up. 'Who are you?'

The young man shrugged. 'My name is Klaus. Does not matter.' His accent was funny. German? Dutch? 'I came to see if you were all right – if you really existed. A McCann who saves the life of another. A miracle surely?'

Now Col was beginning to get angry. He wasn't going to have a stranger come in here and insult his family. 'What do you mean by that?'

'I was there. At the lake. I could not believe what you did. It was very brave.'

Now Col really was angry. 'You were there! Watching. And you didn't help. You're sick, pal.'

The young man shook his head. 'I could do nothing. Believe me. But you did not need help. You were amazing.'

Col raised his voice. 'I did need help. I almost drowned. I'm going to tell the cops about you.'

Klaus shook his head. 'No. Please. No police. Not anyone. I should not be here.' He looked frightened.

'Why shouldn't you be here?' Col asked.

Again Klaus shook his head. 'It is not right that I

should involve—Is that the word? Involve? I should not involve you.' He was backing towards the door. 'I just wanted to make sure you were all right.'

'And what makes you think I won't tell anybody about you? You didn't do anything to help me.'

Klaus stood for a moment by the door. 'Because I think you are a good person,' he said softly.

Then he was gone.

CHAPTER SIX

'Did you have a visitor?'

No chance of a sleep with Dominic in the next room. He pushed open the door carrying a big bunch of grapes and shoved them at Col. 'Want some?'

Col shook his head. 'Did you see him?'

'No. But my mother says she thought you had a visitor. That's why I didn't come in sooner.'

He said it as if Col had been waiting for him. As if he'd be disappointed at having to wait so long. He began to think Dominic was going to be like his shadow from now on.

He decided not to tell Dominic anything about Klaus, and not telling Dominic turned out to be easy. Dominic did all the talking, hardly stopping for breath.

'And when you come out of hospital you're coming to my house. For dinner . . . or for a party. Of course, that means you'll have to meet my sister.' He screwed his face up in disgust. 'Sorry about that. Her name's Ella. Miserella I call her. She's always in a bad mood. She doesn't like you.' He sounded totally shocked by this. 'Even though you saved my life.'

'Maybe that's *why* she doesn't like me.'

Dominic thought that was funny. 'She is a horrible big sister. Really gets on your nerves. Have you got a big sister, Col?' He didn't give Col time to answer. 'It's just your big brother, isn't it? Ella told me. She knows everything about your family.' Dominic stuffed the last of the grapes into his mouth. 'I don't care what she says. You're brilliant. I wish I had a big brother.' He looked around for something else to eat. There was nothing, so he leapt off the bed, ready to go. 'Make sure you get a good night's sleep,' he said, ''cause we've got a big day tomorrow.'

Col leaned up on his pillows. 'What's happening tomorrow?'

'Didn't I tell you? We're being interviewed by the papers. It's OK, my mother will be there as well.' He rolled his eyes. 'Imagine. You and me. We've made the national press, boy!'

Col didn't like that one bit. Neither would Mungo.

Col could refuse to co-operate, but Dominic, eager to spread the word about his 'hero', wouldn't keep his mouth shut.

He dreaded tomorrow.

And sleep didn't rest him. Once again, sleep brought more dreams. Down in that deep, dark water, struggling to get to the surface. His way blocked by ice and demons.

He was glad when morning came, though it was dark with a heavy grey sky that threatened more snow.

Cleo was back on duty, smiling brightly with stories of her baby. 'He is so cute, Col. He just giggles all the time. Do you like babies?'

'You've got to be joking!' Col said at once.

In spite of his lack of sleep he felt brighter today, especially with Nurse Cleo in the room. Today, he was ready to tackle anything, even reporters.

She laughed and studied his temperature. 'Of course you don't. It's not *cool* at your age. But I bet if I brought my little darling in here you'd be goo-gooing along with the rest of them.'

'In your dreams,' he said, but he smiled. Nurse Cleo was like a breath of air as she busied herself about the room, checking charts, tidying his bed.

'Your breakfast's coming. And I'll try to keep Dominic out as long as I can.'

She managed to do that until after breakfast, by which time Col had had a shower and a change of pyjamas.

Dominic came bouncing in like a rubber ball, beaming a big freckle-faced smile.

'I think they're bringing a photographer, so we better look our best.' Dominic spat on his palms and brushed down his unruly hair. 'It's all right for you. You're dead good-looking, Col. I heard Nurse Cleo say that to Miserella.'

Nurse Cleo thought he was dead good-looking! He was really chuffed, and grinned to himself like an idiot. But only for a second, until he realised how stupid he must look with a big daft grin on his face.

The reporter came at eleven, and sure enough there was a photographer with him. Mrs Sampson was there, too, standing by the window, listening quietly to the whole interview.

'I'm Bobby Grant,' the reporter introduced himself, holding out a hand to Col. But Col recognised him. He'd been at their house before, trying to get some dirt on Mungo. If he remembered Col, he didn't show it.

He only opened his notebook and began firing questions right away. Dominic sat cross-legged on the end of the bed, enthusiasm zooming out of him.

'What happened exactly, Col?' Bobby Grant asked.

At first, Col was reticent. Should he tell them about missing school? He did. Should he tell them about being about to steal ten pounds from Dominic's rucksack? He didn't. But when it came to questions about how it felt in that icy loch, suddenly his mouth was too dry to answer. He felt a panic inside even trying to remember it. Dominic made up for him. He was more than eager to fill in the details. The boy was a reporter's dream. Colouring the story so that Col hardly recognised it.

'There I was, thrashing about in the water, my whole life flashing in front of me. Honest. That really happens by the way. I've never wanted my mum so much in my whole life.' He stopped suddenly, and said seriously, 'Don't put that bit in the paper. My friends at school will make my life a misery if you put that in.'

Bobby Grant laughed, and making the most of Dominic's pause asked him, 'When did you first see Col? When did you realise that someone was actually going to save you?' As Dominic opened his mouth to speak the reporter leaned across and touched his hand. 'And slow down, son. I can't write shorthand as fast as you can talk.'

Dominic hesitated, swallowed, and began, slowly at first, but by two sentences he was firing off as rapidly as ever. 'I was going under. And I knew I would never be able to get up again . . . the water was *so* cold. I knew I was going to die and I was scared and then I saw Col and I don't know where he came from, 'cause I hadn't noticed him before but there he was, running at me, pulling off his jacket, and I knew I was going to be OK because Superman was here, that's just what it was like, as if Superman had come to the rescue and I wasn't frightened after that, except . . .' He paused again, swallowed hard, and stared at Col. 'Except when you went under the water and I thought you were going to die instead of me and I couldn't help you. 'Cause I'm not brave like you, Col, or strong, and that's when I was the scaredest and then—whoosh! Suddenly you came roaring up, I couldn't believe it.' Dominic turned back to Bobby Grant. 'But he's here. He's fine . . . he really is Superman.'

Even the photographer laughed. 'You've got a fan, Col.'

'Yeah, how does it feel to be on the side of the good guys for once?' Bobby Grant had the decency to blush as soon as he'd said it. 'Sorry.'

So he did remember him.

Dominic jumped to Col's defence. 'Col couldn't be anything else but a good guy. He'll always be a good guy.'

They finished by taking a photograph. Col and Dominic sitting together on the bed. Col couldn't bring himself to smile despite all their pleadings. He had a bad feeling inside that this would be another mistake. Mungo wouldn't like it. But Dominic smiled enough for both of them, beaming like a rosy apple, tufts of his unruly caramel-coloured hair standing to attention on top of his head.

Suddenly, just before the camera flashed, Dominic gave the thumbs-up sign and beamed his smile at Col. 'See, you, Col . . . you're simply the best.'

That was the picture that appeared in the paper next day, and that was the headline: SIMPLY THE BEST.

And Mungo didn't like it . . . In fact, Mungo was furious.

CHAPTER SEVEN

'That's all I need!' Mungo roared when the story had first appeared. 'My brother on the front pages. Cops'll love that.'

His rage had flowed out of him like a tidal wave. Col couldn't understand why, and told him so.

'You don't understand?' Mungo had roared at him, and yet it seemed to Col he had to search around his brain for an answer. 'You could have died in that loch,' he said finally. 'And for what? . . . Nothing!'

Col thought about bouncy little Dominic, and his tearful parents, and couldn't agree. Though he didn't say so. But he knew it hadn't been for 'nothing'.

'You know I don't like any kind of publicity – especially front-page stuff.'

But Mungo had been on the front pages before now. And this, surely, was good publicity.

In the end it didn't matter why he was so angry. When Col left hospital two days later, Mungo didn't come with Mam to collect him.

'He's waiting for you in the house,' Mam assured him as she packed Col's things into a case. 'We're going to have a nice family dinner. I've made your favourite. Steak pie.'

Steak pie! That was enough to make him almost forget about Mungo.

Nurse Cleo was there, too, fussing around him almost as much as his mother.

'I'm going to miss my good-looking Col,' she said, making him blush. 'Everyone in this hospital is. It's not every day we have a real-life hero in here.'

'Real hero nothing,' Col said, trying to hide his embarrassment. 'I wish everybody would stop calling me that.'

'I'm afraid you'll just have to get used to it, Col. You're a wonderful human being, and you've proved it.' She laughed so heartily Col had to smile. So did Mam.

Would they have smiled if Mungo had been there? Would Nurse Cleo have been so talkative, or would Col have been embarrassed by his brother's patronising attitude towards her?

55

'You must be so proud of him, Mrs McCann.'

Mam beamed, but even now she refused to single out one son for her praise. 'I'm proud of both my boys.'

The Sampsons came in to say goodbye. Dominic had been discharged the day before but had insisted his parents bring him back to see Col.

'He didn't have to coax us too hard,' Mr Sampson pointed out. 'We wanted to see you again to invite you –' his eyes flicked across to Mam '– and your mother, of course, to our house for a celebration meal.'

'It's not to thank you, Col,' Mrs Sampson said quickly. 'Nothing we could ever do would be enough thanks.'

Mrs McCann accepted, but made no arrangements. Not then. It was better if any contact with the Sampsons ended now. Better for Col, better for them. But would it be possible? Not, it seemed, with Dominic around.

'Next week, Col? At the weekend?'

His mother patted his shoulder. 'We'll make arrangements later, Dominic. Let Col get home to his family first.'

The hospital insisted on a wheelchair as he left. It made him feel stupid, being wheeled along when there was nothing wrong with him. He felt fine now. Even the dreams were fading, just as Nurse Cleo had said they would. It was everyone's reaction to him that took him totally by surprise.

As he left, Col was congratulated, and cheered, and as he neared the exit some people even burst into spontaneous applause. He'd never been so embarrassed, or so surprised, in his life.

Dominic, who had insisted on accompanying him, was almost bursting with pride as he strutted along beside him. 'He saved my life, you know,' he'd tell everyone just in case there might be someone who had missed the story. 'I'd be pushing up daisies now if it wasn't for him.'

That made Col laugh. 'I think you might mean water lilies . . . or even ice floes, Dominic.'

Dominic just shrugged. He didn't care. He was basking in the reflected glory around his hero.

Mam had a taxi waiting. When Dominic saw it he started shouting. 'You don't need a taxi. My dad's got the car. We'll take you home.'

But that would be too much for Mungo, arriving home with the Sampsons in tow.

'No thanks, son,' Mam said gently. 'We'll just get off

home in a taxi, and you tell your mum and dad thanks for everything.'

Dominic waved forlornly as they drove off. It was obvious in his bleak expression how much he wished he was going with them.

'You'll have to watch that wee boy,' Mam warned him. 'You'll never be free of him if you're not careful.'

'That's what scares me,' Col admitted.

As they sat in the taxi he asked her, 'Do you think we should go to their house?'

Mam shook her head as if she had already decided. 'Better not, son. The likes of them and the likes of us don't mix. And anyway,' she added, and Col knew this was the real reason, 'Mungo wouldn't like it.'

Mungo was sitting in his chair by the fire when they went in. He didn't stand up to greet Col. He didn't even look up from his paper. 'How's it goin'?'

'Better if you and I were talkin', Mungo,' Col blurted out.

Mungo looked up. For a moment, his expression didn't change. He just stared at his brother and Col braced himself for another angry tirade. It didn't come. Instead, the ghost of a smile crept into Mungo's eyes.

'My fault, Col. Not yours. It was that wee toerag, Dominic, who made sure the press got the story. Cannae keep his gob shut.'

He grabbed Col by the collar and hugged him. An amazing gesture in itself. 'It's good to have you back in the place. If anythin' had happened to you—'

Mungo's eyes were heavy with tears. So were Col's. Mungo suddenly pushed him away and sniffed. 'Hey, you've got me bubbling away here like a lassie.'

Col rubbed his eyes. 'Me too. Hey look, I'm just like our mam at a soppy film.' He gave a melodramatic sob to cover up his own emotion.

Mungo laughed, and his mother rushed at Col, flicking his backside with a dishcloth.

'Don't you dare take the mickey out of me, boy.' She was laughing.

They were all laughing. It was great to be home.

As his mother almost skipped back to the kitchen, happy her boys had made up, she called back over her shoulder, 'Show Col what you got for him, Mungo.'

'You got me a present?'

Mungo opened the cupboard by the fireplace, and took out a cardboard box. 'Here.' He handed the box to Col. 'You've always wanted one of these.'

Col put the box on the coffee table and ripped it open. He gasped. It was a full CD unit, the latest state of the art, the best he had ever seen.

He gazed at Mungo in amazement.

'I told you I'd pay you back for giving me an alibi, didn't I?' Mungo said.

'You bought this for me?'

Mungo hesitated, then he grinned. 'Maybe not exactly *bought*—'

His mother had come back into the living room and caught the last words. She put her hands over her ears. 'Oh, no. I don't want to hear this. You up to your old tricks, Mungo?'

But she was laughing, as if it was only her mischievous son at it again.

Col laughed too. He didn't care where the unit had come from. If someone was stupid enough to get burgled, then they deserved all they got.

CHAPTER EIGHT

Thelma Blaikie was leaning against the school wall, waiting for Col when he went back to school the following Monday. Pretending she wasn't, of course. She was chewing gum, studying her red-painted nails, her black eyes not even looking his way as he moved towards her. He tried to walk past her.

'Ooo, it's *my hero*,' she said.

Col stopped. 'I'm nobody's hero. OK?'

Blaikie blew a bubble. 'Come on, McCann. Front page of the papers and everything.' She smiled. Her teeth looked grey against her too-white face. 'All you need to do now is start wearing your Y-fronts over tights and you really will be Superman.'

Even Col managed a smile at that. 'I do that anyway, Blaikie,' he said, moving away before she could think of a smart answer.

But there *was* something different in the way she spoke to him. As if ever-so-cool Blaikie really was impressed.

It was the same in his classes. His first was Mathematics, and Mrs Holden surprised him more than anyone else.

'We'd like to welcome you back, Col,' she said, when the class had filed in and taken their places.

He glared at her for a second, sure she was taking the mickey. She certainly wasn't smiling. Her face was as grim as it had ever been.

'That was a very brave thing you did,' she went on. 'Someone is alive now, because of *you*.'

A picture of Dominic sprang up before him. Bright, energetic Dominic – all that life still there, because of him?

'You almost died yourself, and yet . . . here you are, still alive. You must be here for a reason. You have made a difference. You have changed the world. That boy may go on to be a great doctor, or a great inventor. To do great things, all thanks to you.' She smiled, a very tight-lipped smile, as if she just wasn't used to it. 'Did you ever see a film called . . . *It's a Wonderful Life*?'

Col slunk down in his chair. He shook his head.

Suddenly, Asim waved his hand wildly. 'I've seen it, Miss. I've seen it.' Without waiting he immediately launched into a potted version of the plot. 'It's about this guy, see, who wishes he was dead, because he's a real loser and then, when he is dead he meets an angel and this angel shows him what might have happened if he'd never been born . . . and he had actually saved his brother's life and his brother would have died if he hadn't been there, and his brother went on to save people's lives as well, so he wasn't that much of a loser after all.' He took a breath. 'Then he wasn't really dead anyway . . .' his voice trailed off. He looked at Mrs Holden. 'Mind you, it was a rubbish angel, Miss. He didn't have wings or anything.'

Mrs Holden looked stunned.

'Sounds really interesting . . .' Col said sarcastically.

'It is a very good résumé of the plot, Asim,' Mrs Holden said, 'and put very succinctly.'

Asim looked puzzled. Not sure what she was talking about or whether she had insulted him or not. Mrs Holden turned her attention back to Col. 'But, like the man in the film, what you have done has changed the world.'

And there it was in her tone, the same tone Col had

heard in Blaikie's. Admiration.

Paul Baxter got to his feet. Paul Baxter, the cleverest boy in school. French, English, Mathematics. He was as good at one as he was at the other. He and Col had hardly broken breath to one another since their first day at school.

'Can I ask Col something, Mrs Holden?'

'Well, of course, Paul. What would you like to ask?'

Col steeled himself. Something sarcastic probably.

Confidently, Paul turned to Col. 'What made you do it?' he asked. 'Because, honestly, I don't think I could ever be that brave.' And he actually looked as if he meant it.

Mrs Holden looked at Col – the whole class did – waiting for his answer.

Col didn't stand up. He slunk even further down in his seat, fiddled with his pencils, tried to think of an answer. 'I wasn't going to at first,' he began. 'It was his own fault. He'd broken the ice himself. I'd watched him banging down a boulder on to it. I heard the ice crack, but I didn't know that's what it was . . . not until I saw him kind of . . . dancing on the ice, sliding into the water. And even then I still thought, *tough. It's your own fault.*'

Col was remembering the icy fog, the stillness, the

cold. 'But he kept shouting for his mam, shouting for somebody to help him and . . . there was only me. I didn't even think. Before I knew it, I was running, knowing I couldn't let him die and that I had to help him.' His voice wavered. 'I'll never really understand why . . .'

He stopped, embarrassed, sure they were all going to laugh at him. But no one did. They were all silent, watching him. Finally, Paul said, 'I think that's brilliant.'

And again, there was real admiration in his voice.

Suddenly, the whole class was talking and laughing and asking questions. Col was the centre of everyone's attention.

As they were filing out at the end of the lesson Mrs Holden called him back. 'I know we've never really got on, but I want you to know how much I applaud what you did, Col. I never thought—' she hesitated, realising what she was just about to say.

Col finished it for her. 'You never thought a McCann would do anything decent.'

She blushed, but she held his gaze. 'Does it not make you feel good?'

Col remembered Bobby Grant's words 'To be on the side of the good guys.'

He wanted to get angry at her, but he couldn't.

Because she was right. He did feel good. 'Better get to my next class,' he said. And then he smiled. *He smiled at Mrs Holden!* 'Us good guys are never late.'

And to his utter surprise, Mrs Holden laughed.

Denny was waiting for him in the corridor. 'Hey, I don't believe it. Was Mrs Holden actually being nice to you?'

Col laughed. 'Sure was.' He didn't add the even more surprising fact . . . that he was being nice to her.

CHAPTER NINE

A few days later Col went back to the loch. Couldn't for the life of him understand why. Mungo had warned him over and over not to go back there – and he certainly didn't want to antagonise Mungo. But even stranger than that was the fact that *he* didn't want to go there. He was frightened to be here. Yet, here he was.

There was still ice on the loch, the weather was as cold as it had been that awful day. He could have gone home after school and sat by the fire listening to his new CD player. Yet, for some reason he couldn't fathom, he walked past his street, up through the estate to the hills and the loch that lay nestled in the valley beyond.

It was beautiful up here. He had always thought so. Beautiful and eerily quiet with dusk falling and the lights of the town twinkling beyond the valley.

Col found himself standing exactly where he had stood that day, watching Dominic jump up and down on the ice. The ice was still broken, and the loch looked strangely peaceful. Would it look as calm, as peaceful, if he had been lying, floating like the reeds, deep down in that icy water? And, suddenly, in spite of the cold he began to sweat. The memory was too much for him to hold in his head. He wanted it away.

Bad idea coming here, boy, he told himself.

'Remembering?'

The voice, so close to his ear, made him jump. He turned so quickly he stumbled and almost fell.

'Sorry. Did I frighten you?'

It was Klaus, the young man who had come to see him in hospital.

'What are you doing here? Did you follow me?'

Klaus shook his head. He badly needed a haircut, Col noticed, and a good wash. 'No. I saw you, I wanted to thank you. You did not tell anyone about me. You did not tell your brother?'

Col snapped at him, 'How do you know so much about my family?'

Klaus shrugged. 'Everyone knows about the McCanns. Especially about your brother.'

'But you're not from round here. You're foreign, ain't ye?'

'I'm Latvian,' Klaus said simply. 'I have been living here for a while, but I am not supposed to be here.'

'What do you mean? Here . . . at the loch? Here . . . in this town?'

Klaus smiled. 'No. Here in this country. I was . . . what do you call them?'

Col knew what Mungo called them. 'Dirty illegal immigrants, them and asylum seekers. Bleedin' this country dry. They should all get chucked back to where they belong.'

'You're an illegal immigrant?'

Mungo and his mates made life hell for the asylum seekers on a nearby estate. What would he do if he found out that an illegal immigrant was up here, alone? An illegal immigrant with no protection at all from the police? The thought made Col shiver.

'I paid a lot of money to come to Britain,' Klaus went on. 'Everything I had. Transported in a crowded, dirty lorry with so many others. I was promised work. Peace too. So much poverty in my country. In my village, I have a mother, sisters. I came to find work.'

'But why Scotland? Why here?'

Klaus crouched down and began picking at the icy ferns. 'When we arrived it was up to every one of us to find somewhere to live, to hide, a place where we could disappear. Most of my comrades stayed in English towns. They thought I was mad to come here. I thought there might be others here in this town, like me, illegal immigrants. But no . . . I am the only one from Latvia. I stayed here because Scotland with its mountains and its lochs seemed so much like my own country. I thought, even alone, I would not be so homesick here.'

'You look pretty sick to me, Klaus, son,' Col said, suddenly feeling sorry for the young man in front of him. The feeling took him by surprise. He had always been like Mungo, hating them. He had always taken his lead from his brother.

'Why are you telling me all this?' Col was puzzled. 'You're taking a chance. If I told my brother about you, he would bring his mates up here. They don't like your kind. Boy, you would be sorry.'

Klaus looked at Col for a long time. His eyes were a muddy blue and he didn't blink – not once. 'I don't think you will. I trust you.'

Here was another first for Col. Someone actually trusted him.

'I came here thinking I would find friends, someone to help me. Instead, I found only violence and hate. Just like at home.' Klaus almost smiled when he said that. 'I had lost all hope. I could find hardly any work, only odd jobs with the farmers around here. Always waiting for the police to find me, always hiding. I had had enough. I have wanted to go back home for so long.' He closed his eyes. For a second Col thought he might be about to cry. Please, don't let him cry, he thought. He wouldn't know how to handle that.

But Klaus didn't cry. Suddenly, his eyes snapped open and he looked at Col and said with real fervour, 'I still want to go back home, but I don't know how. I can't trust anyone. When you ran into that icy water and you saved the little boy, you risked your life. You gave me back my hope, Col, that there is still decency somewhere. I know I can trust you.'

Col's breath clouded the cold air in nervous bursts. *He'd* done that?

'You've come across Mungo before. That's how you know about us.' Col knew it suddenly. Mungo and his mates roaming the area, ready to do battle with anyone who was different. Klaus the foreigner would fit that perfectly.

'I had been warned to watch out for him. Yes,' he answered softly.

'How do you live?' Col asked, trying to imagine how it would be with no friends, no money, no food.

Klaus seemed to take a long time to answer.

'Some of the farmers around here give me work, no questions asked. I sleep anywhere.' He gestured across the loch. 'The old air-raid shelters around there are good hiding places.'

'You live there?' Col screwed up his face in disgust. The old wartime shelters, embedded in the moorland, where the townspeople used to take shelter during the Blitz, were manky, smelly places. 'You better be careful. Everybody knows about them. They'll find you eventually.'

Klaus smiled. His teeth were small and white and even, except the front ones were broken. Not many dentists in Latvia. Not a lot of time to think about your teeth, Col supposed. 'I'll be careful. Don't worry.'

Col stood up to go. 'I'm not worried. You're not my problem.'

Klaus only smiled again. 'You know, maybe that day you didn't just save Dominic's life. Maybe you were sent to help me too.'

* * *

Col wandered home in the icy darkness. He'd never go back to the loch again, he decided. He knew he couldn't. Not with Klaus there. If Mungo ever discovered there was an illegal immigrant sleeping rough there, Col didn't even want to think about what he would do.

In that moment he knew Klaus was right. He wouldn't tell his brother about him. It wouldn't be a lie. He would never lie to his brother. He'd only hold it back, for Mungo's own good. Mungo would only get himself into trouble if he knew.

At least, he told himself that was the reason.

Mrs Macann, who lived down the street from Col, was opening her front door as he passed.

His family didn't talk to the Macanns. They were no relation, the names were not even spelt the same, but Mrs Macann and Col's mother had more than one stormy argument because of that. Mrs Macann had even removed the nameplate from her door because of the number of visits the police made to her house thinking she was 'one of them McCanns'. Consequently, there was a long-time feud between the two families. And Mungo took every opportunity of breaking the odd window in her house, scraping keys across her car as it stood parked at their front door, of doing any irritating little thing he could think of to ensure the bad feeling remained.

Col began to hurry past her. Didn't want an argument.

'Col?' she shouted after him.

He stopped and turned defiantly. He was expecting to be blamed for something, or warned about something, or asked to pass on some insult to his mother. He put on his surly *I'm a McCann* expression. 'Aye? What do you want?'

'I just wanted to tell ye . . . that was a wonderful thing you done, son. Wonderful.'

Col thought she was taking the mickey. But she went on, 'The whole street thinks the same thing. They might not say it – with your brother you don't know how it might be taken – but . . . the whole street thinks it was wonderful.'

Then she was gone. Her door closed softly. He was alone on the dark street with only a mangy dog for company, barking in some alley.

The whole street was proud of him, and his class, and Mrs Holden, and . . .

What was happening?

CHAPTER TEN

Col had never been so nervous in his life, and he was annoyed at himself for feeling like that. After all, he was only going to the Sampsons' house for a meal. They'd been inviting him for almost a fortnight – Dominic phoning him up, pleading with him. Inviting his mother too. Her answer was immediate.

'Me? Go to their house? Not on your life. And I'd advise you to steer well clear of them, Col. I know they mean well, but . . .'

She let the 'but' drift off. Col understood what she meant – Mungo didn't want him to go. Mungo wanted the whole drama to be put firmly in the past where it belonged. The Sampsons lived in a different world. A world Col could never fit into.

Dominic's parents would have let it rest, understanding Col's reluctance, but Dominic just wouldn't take no for an answer.

'Just this once,' he pleaded on the phone. 'I'll never ask you again, I promise. But I want to show you my PlayStation. I've got brilliant games. We could play them.'

In the end, it was curiosity as well as Dominic's pleas that made him change his mind. 'Just this once,' Col told a jubilant Dominic. That was what he told his mother too. 'Just this once.'

She declined the invite. It was her favourite bingo night, she said, but the truth was she didn't want to annoy Mungo. She did buy Col a new sweater for the visit though. 'Nobody's goin' to say my boy's not well dressed.'

He walked across town to Dominic's house despite Dominic's frantic insistence that 'My dad'll come and get you'.

But Col had been just as insistent. He'd walk. March had burst into life with a warm temperature and a promised early spring.

'I've just seen my first crocus,' his mother had said as he was leaving. 'That means we'll have a good summer.'

Which was probably the kiss of death to any good weather. Mam, they had discovered long ago, was totally rubbish at predicting the weather. Whatever she said, they usually ended up with the opposite.

It was a crisp, dry afternoon as he walked through the town centre and up into the west end where Dominic lived. The Sampsons' house was situated in a quiet tree-lined terrace with fancy cars in all the driveways, and well-tended gardens.

Dominic was watching for him and came leaping down the front steps and whizzing towards him. 'You're just in time. Everybody's here.' He lowered his voice. 'Even Miserella. Bet you 10p you can't make her smile.'

He was pulling at Col's sleeve, hurrying him into the house. 'Come on! Come on!'

Mrs Sampson appeared at the door. 'Dominic. Leave Col be for a minute.' She flicked at his backside with a dishcloth, and Dominic yelped. Just what Col's mother did to him. Maybe they weren't so different after all. The thought cheered him up. He smiled as Mrs Sampson led him in to meet the rest of the family. The hall-way was almost as big as his front room, with an ornate winding staircase leading up to the floors above. A dark wood unit took up all of one wall and it was filled with expensive-looking china and silver and crystal. Col tried to take it all in so he could describe it to Mam later. The Chinese rug, the crystal chandelier, the paintings. In the dining room, Mr Sampson was opening a bottle of wine. He turned and smiled, a genuine smile. This family really seemed to like him.

And, of course, he knew why. He had saved their son's life. Col glanced at Dominic. He was gazing at Col as if he were some kind of superhero. Yet, if it hadn't been for Col he would be deep down in the dark waters of the loch. He could almost picture his white face, bloated, floating . . .

Too scary! Too much like being back down there himself.

'Are you OK, Col?' Mrs Sampson asked. 'You've gone quite pale.'

He shook the memory away, though it continued to cling around the corners of his mind like a spider's web.

Mrs Sampson led him into the living room. 'You haven't met our daughter yet, Col. This is Ella.' And she pulled a reluctant female into view.

Ella was slightly taller than Col, with long hair, the same nutty colour as Dominic's, and eyes as icy as the loch. Miserella matched her name perfectly, Col thought. She looked as if she were smelling something awful . . . and it was probably him.

'Now, you three get to know each other and I'll call you when dinner's ready.'

Mrs Sampson flashed a warning look at Ella as she passed her on the way to the kitchen. Col didn't miss it. It was a you-be-nice-to-him-or-else kind of look. And, as soon as the door of the kitchen was closed, Ella ignored it.

'Before we go any further,' she said, 'the furniture has been screwed down and we've counted the silver.'

Dominic jumped at her. 'You said you'd be nice to Col. You promised. I'm going to tell Mum and Dad on you.'

Col held him back from rushing from the room. 'Don't bother with her, Dominic. She's just jealous.'

He decided to look at her the same way she was looking at him, as if she were the bad smell.

'What made you save his life? Think there would be a reward?'

She was trying to rile him, to make him angry. She thought it was going to be easy. Col decided he wasn't going to let her.

'Meeting you is reward enough for me.'

She hadn't expected that. In fact, Col hadn't intended

to say it. But, all the same, it was just the right thing.

Ella's mouth hung open for a second, then suddenly she was laughing. Not the I'm-having-a-wonderful-time kind of laughing. But more your insulted kind of laughter, because she was stuck for words. 'You have some nerve!' she managed to say.

Col held out his hand to Dominic. 'Does that count as a smile? Do you owe me 10p?'

Dominic giggled. '10p? You deserve 20p for that. Round one to you, Col.'

Miserella's eyes narrowed. She made a grab for her brother, but he darted behind Col. 'What was your bet? Tell me, you little horror!'

Dominic began jumping out on either side of Col chanting, 'Make me! Make me!'

No wonder she was annoyed, but they didn't tell her. And that only made her even more miserable.

'Our secret,' Dominic mouthed at her.

While they waited for dinner Dominic insisted Col go up to see his PlayStation. Col had expected it to be a better one, more expensive, but he didn't show that to Dominic. He was too proud of it. 'I paid for this myself you know. I've got a paper round, and Mum and Dad give me money for any odd jobs I do around the house.

Dad said if I saved up so much, he would give me the rest.'

Col was surprised at that. 'He made you save up for it yourself?' He would have thought with the money the Sampsons had, his dad would have given him anything he wanted. But it didn't seem to bother Dominic.

'Oh yes. My dad says you appreciate things better if you've got to work for them.' He hugged his Play-Station and laughed. 'And I definitely appreciate this.'

He even made Col laugh.

He began dancing about with excitement, as if he needed the toilet. 'Want to play? I've got lots of games.'

They played until Mrs Sampson shouted on them for dinner. Col had to promise to come back up again before he went home.

'Him and that PlayStation, Col,' Mr Sampson said when they came downstairs. He ruffled Dominic's hair at that, but Dominic shook him away. He didn't want Col to see him treated like a 'wee boy'.

All in all, Col had a better time than he expected. He laughed quite a lot and, annoying as he was, Dominic was funny. Keeping the company going with a series of knock-knock jokes which Dominic found far funnier than anyone else. It was very clear that he was the apple, in fact, the whole orchard of his parents' eyes. They teased him, laughed with him. Dominic, the smallest in the room, filled the house with his vitality.

And all the time Col was thinking: if it hadn't been for him, they would be mourning for him, now, missing him, grieving for him. If it hadn't been for him.

He remembered Mrs Holden's words, 'You might have saved the life of a great doctor . . . ' and he asked Dominic, 'What do you want to be when you grow up?'

No hesitation. 'Och, that's easy. I want to work in a chip shop. Imagine making fish and chips for a living!'

Ella groaned. 'You have no ambition, Dominic.'

Col only laughed. 'It's good to know I saved your life for something worthwhile.'

That made them all laugh, although Dominic wasn't quite sure what he was laughing at. All of them, except Ella.

She continued to watch Col, distrustfully, throughout the meal.

'You haven't put arsenic in my soup or anything?' he whispered to her.

'If only I'd thought of it,' she whispered back.

The soup was nothing to write home about. It was watery and dark and looked more like something you washed your dishes in. And it had bits of fried bread floating in it too.

'They're called *croûtons*, cretin,' Miserella told him smugly as he pushed them around his bowl.

Nothing like as good as the thick, meaty broths his mam made. She'd be pleased when he told her that later.

When the meal was finished, Mr Sampson got to his feet. For one awful moment Col thought he was going to make a speech.

But he didn't. Not really. He lifted his glass to Col, and thanked him once again for saving Dominic.

'And remember, Col. If there's ever anything you need – *anything* – just ask. We'll always be here for you, the way you were there for our son.'

Dominic groaned. 'Aw, Dad. Don't go on. This is so embarrassing.'

Mr Sampson laughed. 'I know. Point taken. Shut up, Dad. I'm just going to announce one more thing, and then I'll shut up for the night. I promise.' He looked at Col with almost as much fondness as he had looked at Dominic. 'Because of what you did we put you forward for an award, and next month we've all been invited to London to attend the ceremony. Col, you're going to receive The Young People's Act of Courage Award.'

CHAPTER ELEVEN

'Congratulations, Col – on the award – it's wonderful news.' Mrs Holden had sought him out in the corridor at school.

Everyone was congratulating him. From his own classmates, right up to the headmaster. And now, surprise, surprise, even Mrs Holden.

'It's an honour for the school, too,' she told him.

'I don't know whether I'll go,' he said sullenly.

'But you must go, Col. An all-expenses-paid trip to London. Meeting so many interesting people . . .' She paused, and added as if it surprised her as much as Col, 'People as brave as yourself.'

'It's just not my scene,' he said, and walked away from her.

They all thought he should go, everyone, even Blaikie who had beamed at him as he had come in through the school gates that morning.

'You're so lucky, Col. I wish I could go to London. Can I fit in your case?'

Even Paul Baxter hurried towards him. 'Col, any chance of you writing something about your trip for the school magazine? It would make a great story.'

'Do I look like a reporter?' he had snapped back.

But in spite of that, something had changed in Paul's attitude towards him. He wouldn't let it go. 'Maybe we could do an interview when you come back. Congratulations, by the way.'

And he had patted Col on the back and moved off.

Col wanted to be angry, wanted Paul Baxter to know he was angry. He was a McCann. He wasn't the type to be patted on the back and congratulated by the likes of him. He wanted to run after him, challenge him to a fight. Instead, he just stood there in the playground glaring.

Only Denny understood. 'Your Mungo won't like it. Back in the papers again, eh?'

And that was the worst part. Denny was right.

When Col had gone home from the Sampsons and told his brother about the award, Mungo had leapt to his feet, angrier than Col had ever seen him. 'Do that family never give up? You're no' goin' and that's that!'

Col had already decided he wasn't going because he knew the trouble it would cause. But Mungo ordering him not to go only got his back up.

'What's your problem with this, Mungo?' he shouted at him. 'It's a free trip to London.'

'See! You've changed already. You want to go to London! I'll take ye to London. What do you want to go with the Sampsons for? Think they're better than us? Is that it?'

Col thought he understood then. Mungo was afraid, afraid that seeing how the Sampsons lived would make him prefer them to his own family.

'You and Mam can come as well, they said. I've already said I would only go if you two came. You're my family.'

Mungo sneered at that. 'Me and Mam go anywhere wi' that bunch? You have got to be kiddin'. I knew this wouldn't be the end of it. I just knew it.'

And it wasn't.

The very next night, Bobby Grant came knocking at their door.

'What the hell do you want?' Mam said angrily as

soon as she saw him.

'Keep your hair on, Mrs McCann. For once, it's not Mungo I'm here to see. It's your son Col. Hero of the hour. For once, I'm going to be able to say something nice about your family.'

He didn't get another word out. From somewhere inside the house there was a fierce battlecry and Mungo suddenly appeared and dived at the reporter. He was caught totally unawares. One second he was standing on the doorstep, and the next he was tumbling down their front steps locked in a wrestling hold with Mungo.

Mungo had him on the ground, and was ready to pound a fist into his face. It was only Mam who stopped him. 'Mungo! For goodness sake let him go!' she screamed at him as she ran down the steps to pull them apart. 'Help me, Col.'

Together, they managed to wrench the struggling Mungo to his feet.

Bobby Grant sat on the ground and rubbed his chin. He had a smarmy, insolent smile on his face. 'You're always good for a story, Mungo.'

Mungo snarled back at him. 'Don't get on the wrong side of me, Bobby-boy. I can make you very sorry.'

Bobby Grant scoffed at the threat. 'You're a small-time thug, Mungo. Nothing else. Who do you think you are? Al Capone?'

That really made Mungo angry and he struggled to get to him, but Mam and Col held him fast.

'He's no' worth it, Mungo,' Col said.

The brawl had alerted the neighbours. Some peeked out of their doors, or drew net curtains back warily to see the cause of the commotion – only to step back in, hide quickly, when they saw that Mungo was involved.

'You think I'm a small-time crook? Ha! You know nothin'! Nothin'!' Mungo yelled. 'You wait and see!'

Mam stood between her sons and the reporter. 'Be on your way. You'll not get a story here this night.'

He did though. The next day there was a piece about the award, and the brawl. It also said the McCanns were not available for comment.

More trouble from Mungo, and his mother wasn't any help.

'They can send you the award. You don't have to go,' she said.

Added to everything else, winter rushed back with a vengeance, and the nights were once again bone-crushingly cold.

Col remembered Klaus in one of the air-raid shelters

up by the loch. He'd be freezing, and probably hungry.

He sat by the fire after tea one night toasting his toes, and exhausted after another tirade from Mungo about the story in the paper. His mother had gone off to her bingo, but Col couldn't stop thinking about Klaus.

He could still smell his mother's broth, still feel its warmth in his stomach. I bet Klaus could fair go some of that broth, he thought.

Mungo would never know. Col knew now he would never risk Mungo following him, or finding out about Klaus.

He didn't want to leave the fire, but at least, he consoled himself, he had the fire to look forward to when he came home.

He filled a flask with soup, stuffed some bread in a bag and, as an afterthought, an old duvet his mother was always planning to take to the homeless hostel in town.

As he made his way up towards the loch, Col worried about how he would find Klaus. But he needn't have. Klaus found him, as he stood once more transfixed at the spot where he had saved Dominic – all the fears, all the terror rushing back at him.

'I'm mad to come here,' he told Klaus. 'When I come

here, I'm back in that water again. Freezing, and frightened and . . .' He shivered.

'Then why did you come?' Klaus asked.

He looked even paler, Col thought. Paler, thinner, and more unkempt.

In answer, Col shoved the bag with the duvet and the flask in it at him. 'Here, I brought you these. It's one blinkin' cold night.'

Klaus sounded puzzled. 'You brought me this? Why?'

He didn't know why. He couldn't answer that. It wasn't like him. He shrugged. 'Maybe I lost my brain when I fell in that loch.'

'Maybe you found yourself,' Klaus said in a soft voice.

'Don't talk wet,' Col groaned.

Klaus smiled. 'You're not a bit like your brother.'

Col jumped angrily to his defence. 'Don't you say a word about my brother. He's the best.'

'He hates my kind,' Klaus reminded him.

'Why should he no'? You come here. Take our jobs, live off us. Why don't you just go back to your own country?'

He heard himself repeating exactly what he always heard Mungo saying.

'I want to, Col. You don't know how much I want to,'

Klaus said.

'So, why don't you?'

Klaus shoved his hands deep into the pockets of his anorak and shivered. Col saw fear in his face, and thought he understood why.

'You're frightened they wouldn't send you home. They'd put you in jail. Is that it?' Col thought of him in his cold, dungeon hideaway. 'Even jail's got to be better than this.'

Klaus shook his head. 'Not jail, Col. I've never done anything wrong in my life. I only wanted to make money for my family.'

'But, you can't stay here for ever.'

'I don't want to,' Klaus said. His face brightened. 'Maybe you can help me get home.'

That made Col laugh. 'Me? I can't even help myself. I've not got any money.'

'You helped Dominic and you didn't have any money.'

Col laughed. 'Jump in the loch then, and I'll fish you out.'

Klaus managed a faint smile. He was a foreigner, Col thought. Probably didn't share his sense of humour.

Klaus took him to the shelter where he was hiding out. It was dirty and damp and icy cold. Klaus wrapped himself in the duvet and told Col all about himself, the village where he came from, all about his family. His mother, who laughed a lot. His sisters, one who wanted to marry and have plenty of babies, and the other who wanted a career and beautiful clothes like the models she saw in tattered magazines.

'They want a good life, Col. Like everyone else in the world.' It seemed to Col that he told him every detail about his life. So long, Col thought, since he'd talked to anyone about it, and had anyone to listen. And Col told him about the award, and the trip to London.

'Why don't you go?' Klaus asked him. 'It would be an adventure.'

'That's what my teacher says. But I can't. Mungo wouldn't like it. My mother wouldn't come with me. And I'm not going with them by myself.' He paused. 'Anyway, I don't want to go.'

Klaus stared at him for a long while, saying nothing. 'But you do,' he said at last.

And Col knew it was true. He did want to go to London.

But Mungo would never let him.

CHAPTER TWELVE

'If Col doesn't want to go, Dominic, you'll just have to accept it.' Mrs Sampson had been trying to placate her son since Col had phoned to tell them his decision.

'But he does want to go,' Dominic insisted, then added, 'He told me, he's desperate to go.'

Ella tutted loudly. 'What a liar!'

'Ella!' Mrs Sampson scolded.

Dominic turned on his sister. 'It's all your fault. You don't want him to go. You don't like him.'

'That's true,' Ella admitted. 'I don't want him to go, and I don't like him. I don't trust him.' She pleaded with her mum. 'They're a dangerous family, mother. They're always in the newspaper. His dad was notorious as well. He was killed driving a getaway car.'

'I know their reputation,' Mrs Sampson conceded. 'But that makes no difference. Col saved Dominic's life.

He'll always be special to me.'

Dominic stuck his tongue out at his sister. He leapt at his mother. 'If you asked him, Mum, he would go. Please, Mum! Can we go and see Col?'

Ella screeched at him, 'You're not going to that house. We could have a lovely trip to London . . . just us. I'll make a cardboard cut out of Col McCann. I'll even sit beside it.'

'Shut up you!' Dominic yelled. 'If Col doesn't go to London, neither do I!'

Ella smiled. 'This trip is sounding better by the minute.'

It was only because of Dominic that Mrs Sampson found herself knocking on the door of the McCanns' house. Dominic was in tow of course. He had refused to stay at home.

She hoped the notorious Mungo would not be there, but to her dismay it was Mungo himself who opened the door.

He spread himself in the doorway, his whole body language barring their way.

'What do you want?'

Before Mrs Sampson could answer, Dominic, who

couldn't read body language too well, had caught sight of Col and darted under Mungo's arm.

'Hey, Col,' he shouted. 'It's me!'

'I'd never have guessed,' Col said, coming towards him.

'Dominic!' Mrs Sampson tried to call him back but it was no use, he was in now. 'Sorry,' she said to Mungo.

It was only when Mam hurried from the kitchen that Mungo moved aside sullenly.

'Oh, Mrs Sampson, it's yourself. Come on in, would you like a wee cup of tea?'

Col was glad his mother greeted them so warmly. He wanted the Sampsons to know that his family was special too. In spite of all they had heard.

'I've just made some pancakes,' Mam said.

'My Mam makes the best pancakes,' Col said proudly.

'I'm sure she does, Col,' Mrs Sampson smiled. 'I've never mastered the art of making them myself.'

Mam ushered them into her living room, and switched off the television.

Mungo stood leaning against the doorway, silently, just watching. His face giving nothing away.

'If you've come to try to persuade me to go, I'm not going,' Col glanced at his brother as if to reassure him.

'Well, if you're not going, I'm not going.' Dominic

flopped on to the sofa in a huff. 'There's no point if you don't go.'

Mrs Sampson sat beside him and patted his knee. She looked at Col. 'You know what he's like, Col. This is all he goes on about. He's driving the whole family potty. I promised I'd come and ask you just one more time. But he is right. There is no point if you don't go.'

Col looked at her. She was a really pretty woman, in a pale sort of a way, but in the light from the fire she had a golden glow. Her golden hair, her gold earrings, the gold necklet she wore, her gold watch, all gleamed in the firelight and seemed to make her come alive. Mungo was watching her too. Probably thinking exactly what Col was thinking. Mrs Sampson was pretty, beautiful even, but she wasn't a patch on his Mam. His Mam, with her beautiful eyes and her rich, warm laughter. She was laughing now, smiling at Dominic.

'Yes, I've heard some tales about you, Dominic,' she said.

'Please let him go, Mrs McCann.'

'I'm not stoppin' him, darlin'.' She turned to Col. 'Am I, son?'

Her glance took in Mungo. As if she was waiting for him to say something. Mungo didn't. He remained stonily silent and sombre by the doorway. Mrs Sampson didn't wait for Col's answer. 'We all want Col with us. We'll be flown down and put up in a lovely hotel, and you, and . . . .' She glanced up. 'Mungo, of course, I'm sure you'd both enjoy it.'

'No' me,' Mungo declared coldly.

Dominic shot forward. 'It would be great. It would be brilliant. It would be a laugh a minute.'

Col tried to say he didn't want to go. But he couldn't find the words. He *did* want to go. He'd never wanted to go anywhere so much.

His mother hesitated, too. And with that ever so slight hesitation, Col knew his mother wanted him to be there. But she knew it would cause friction between her boys and that was what she wanted to avoid more than anything.

To Col's astonishment it was Mungo who spoke up. 'You know, Col, maybe you should go. It would be a great experience for you and I wouldn't want to hold you back from that.'

Col swallowed. Was he hearing right? 'Do you really mean that?'

Dominic leapt to his feet shouting, 'Col's coming to London!'

His mother pulled him back down, but she was beaming with pleasure.

They do really want me there, Col thought. It isn't just Dominic, it's Mrs Sampson too.

Mungo was nodding his head. 'Naw, Col. You go. You can't turn down somethin' like that.'

That was all the encouragement Mam needed. 'I think it might be good for Col as well. As you so rightly say, Mungo, an experience.'

Now, Col managed a smile. 'You'll enjoy it, Mam. London. You can go to the shops there.' He looked at Mrs Sampson. 'My Mam loves shopping.'

But Mam was already shaking her head. 'No. Not me, Col. I'm not a great one for travelling. I never go on holidays or anything.' She looked at Mrs Sampson. 'I know Col will be fine with you.'

And nothing Col said would persuade her to change her mind. Mungo joined in the plans and listened to all the talk of travel arrangements and hotels. Col had seldom seen him so affable. When they had finished, he rubbed his hands together. 'Right, Mam, what about those pancakes then?'

It turned out to be a very enjoyable afternoon. Mungo was at his very best, and their Mam had Mrs Sampson giggling with laughter with her tales of bingo.

By the time they left it had all been arranged. Col would go to London with the Sampsons.

* * *

'What made you change your mind, bruv?' Col asked Mungo later. 'I mean, you were so against it, and then, suddenly . . .'

Mungo only shrugged. 'They seemed OK. She seems really nice, actually. And she's right. There isn't any point if you don't go.' He smiled. 'You really did want to go all the time, didn't ye?'

'No, if it meant us two fallin' out.'

Mungo patted him on the back. 'Good boy.'

'Good boy indeed,' Mam said. 'Nothing should ever come between you two boys.'

She looked long and hard at Col.

'What are you thinking, Mam?' he asked.

'I'm thinking about what you're going to wear at this do.'

Col had got a new suit for his granny's funeral only last year. 'I'll wear that,' he said.

His mother shook her head. 'No, indeed. You're not wearing a funeral suit to something like that. No. I'll tell you what you're going to wear.'

She hesitated dramatically. Col waited.

'You're going to wear the kilt,' she said.

CHAPTER THIRTEEN

'I am glad you are going. You did really want to go, didn't you?'

Klaus sat on a box in the shelter, his face hidden in the shadows. Col couldn't understand how he could live here and he told him so.

'I have no choice, Col.'

'But it's horrible and it's smelly and it's . . .' Col blew a cloud of breath into the dark air. '*So* cold.'

It was all of these things, and more. It was scary.

This time, Col had brought Klaus sandwiches and some left-over chicken. 'But I've got to take the flask back. Mam missed it.'

Klaus had the duvet wrapped around him. 'This too?'

Col thought he looked comical wearing the red-checked duvet. 'No. Forget that. I'll tell her I took it to Oxfam.'

'Do you wish your mother was going with you?' Klaus asked him.

'I sometimes think you're a mind reader,' Col said. 'Yeah. I wish she was. I wish someone was. Somebody, just for me. But . . .' He hesitated, because he didn't want to talk about his mother. It was as if he was betraying her. 'But I understand. My mam's really quite shy. I mean, she kids on she's loud and dead cheery and everything, but she gets really nervous meeting new people. And she's scared stiff of flyin'.'

But he didn't really believe that. His mam always preferred to be with Mungo. Her favourite. He hated to admit it, but had always accepted it. Until now, when he wanted her with *him* so much.

Klaus was smiling, there in the shadows. He didn't look well, Col thought, watching him. It couldn't be good for him sleeping on a cold stone floor night after night. 'I think you should go to the cops, Klaus.'

Klaus was suddenly on his feet, the duvet slipping to the floor. 'No, Col! Promise me you won't tell about me. I trust you.'

Col was offended. 'I'm hardly likely to tell on you after all this time, am I?'

Klaus smiled again. 'It's nice you worry about me,

Col. You're the only friend I have made since I came here. The only one I do trust. I'll find a way to get home, you wait and see.'

Col stood up, too, ready to go. 'You'll be careful while I'm away?' He was thinking of Mungo, roaming the streets at night, looking for trouble. Imagining him wandering up here, finding Klaus. Why should he be so worried about Klaus? Yet, he was.

'I will be very careful,' Klaus assured him. 'When are you off to London?'

'Next Monday, and I bet I have some great stories to tell you when I get back.'

The atmosphere in the London hotel was electric. On the ground floor, a massive function room was being set up for the award ceremony that evening. Television cameras were already in place, the whole hotel was buzzing.

'Highlights on BBC News,' Mr Sampson told them. 'One of their top newsreaders is the master of ceremonies.'

Their rooms were on the third floor. Dominic and Col were sharing the room adjacent to Mr and Mrs Sampson, and Ella was in a single room down the hall.

'It's not fair,' she moaned. 'My room's not half as nice

as theirs. And I'm stuck away down there on my own. Why couldn't I have brought a friend?'

'Because you've not got any.' Dominic smirked, and Ella kicked him.

'Ella! You're lucky you came at all. It was only supposed to be Col and Dominic. We insisted you come too, and we had to pay for you. So shut up and enjoy yourself.' Mr Sampson refused to take Ella seriously. He was in a great mood, humming as he unpacked, looking forward to every minute of this trip, determined everyone should enjoy it to the full.

'This is such a wonderful time for us,' he confided to Col when he was in the boys' room helping Dominic put his clothes away. 'Things for us could have been so tragically different, if it hadn't been for you, Col. So, I'm not going to let anything spoil it.'

Dominic came running from the en suite bathroom. 'Come and see the size of this, Col. It's humungous. And we've got two toilets!'

Col burst out laughing. So did Mr Sampson. 'Two toilets! What am I going to do with that boy?'

They were to be ready for the reception downstairs at seven o'clock. With three males in kilts to get ready,

Mrs Sampson was running from one to the other. There were ties to be knotted, and laces to be tied. At one point, Mr Sampson trooped into the boys' room in disgust. 'Look at that!' He held out the ceremonial dagger that slid into the sock. 'A plastic skean-dhu! Can you believe it!'

Mrs Sampson laughed. 'William Wallace wouldn't have done much damage with that.'

Ella was behind him, still trying to help with his tie. She sneered at Col. 'In your case, I can see the point of a plastic skean-dhu. Much safer for everyone.'

Col said nothing. The skean-dhu tucked into his sock was the real thing. Ice cold steel.

'Somebody's going to have to help me,' Dominic wailed. He came out of the bathroom, still in his underwear and carrying his kilt. 'I haven't a clue how to put this on.'

Miraculously, they were all ready in time. Mrs Sampson looked stunning in a pale blue beaded dress and, Col had to admit, even Miserella looked pretty good. Her dress was silky and short and if she could only manage a smile, she might even look as stunning as her mother.

Mrs Sampson stood back to survey the three men.

She beamed with pride. 'You all look wonderful,' she said, smiling especially at Col. 'My Col, you do look handsome in a kilt.'

Ella sniggered. 'Yes, you should wear a frock more often.'

Col wouldn't get annoyed at her. He had decided to take a leaf out of Mr Sampson's book. He was excited and wanted to savour every moment. Anyway, he had a feeling that Ella wasn't as miserable as she pretended to be. That she was just as excited at the thought of tonight as he was.

There was a host of celebrities at the Act of Courage Awards. Dominic was overwhelmed.

'I've seen that one on TV. What's her name?' He pointed out a red-haired glamour girl, who was wearing a dress with no back to it.

Mrs Sampson tutted when she saw it. 'Wearing a dress like that! This is a children's award ceremony, after all.'

Dominic grew even more excited. 'Look! That's the one who does the gardening programme!'

Famous faces flitted in and out of the crowd, smiling, talking, shaking hands.

Suddenly, Ella was jumping up and down with excitement. 'It's my favourite band. They're here. All of them. They're totally gorgeous!'

Col followed her gaze to a smarmy-looking group of boys. He thought they looked stupid, not gorgeous. She let out a series of excited yells. For once she forgot to be cool. 'I've got to get their autographs. I've got to!'

Col and Dominic looked at each other. 'Is she embarrassing, or what?' Dominic said.

The round tables in the function room were festooned with flowers and balloons and at the far end a stage with microphones and a lectern stood ready for the presentations after the meal.

The meal they were treated to was sumptuous. Melon, and soup, and peach sorbet, and the angry-eyed salmon that was laid on the table for the main course seemed to stare straight at Col. 'It looks as if it's ready to eat me!' Col laughed.

The meal, however, didn't suit Dominic. 'Could I get pie and chips?' he asked a waiter.

Ella was mortified. 'Pie and chips! We can't take you anywhere.'

But the waiter only laughed and whispered to Dominic, 'Tonight, nothing's a problem. I'll make sure you get your pie and chips.'

And he did.

'He must be under the impression that you're the hero,' Ella told him sarcastically.

'He's really nice. I like him,' Dominic said.

Just then, the BBC newsreader who was hosting the event announced that after a short interval the awards would be presented.

'That's what I want to be when I grow up,' Dominic said, dreamily.

'A BBC newsreader?' Col asked.

'No. A waiter,' Dominic corrected him. 'I think that would be a brilliant job. You would meet so many interesting people.'

Col laughed so much Ella looked at him suspiciously. Now I've saved the life of a future waiter, he thought to himself.

Col was amazed when the award ceremony began in earnest. One by one, as their deeds were extolled by the newsreader, each young hero strode up to the stage to tumultuous applause and was awarded their trophy by a chosen celebrity.

The boy who, in spite of being badly injured himself, had saved his father from freezing to death by going for the mountain rescue team when his father was injured. The girl whose face was scarred for life because she ran back into a burning building to save her sister, then threw her down to waiting firemen before being rescued herself.

Could he have done that?

No. That was real bravery. What he had done wasn't brave. He hadn't even wanted to save Dominic. He had been prepared to let him drown, let him die in that icy loch. He had even been on the verge of stealing from him. How ashamed he was of that now. No. What he had done he'd done without thinking. It had been as natural as snapping your hand away from a window as it was about to slam shut on your fingers.

No. What he'd done wasn't brave. But this, all of this, was bravery.

He felt ashamed. He shouldn't be here. He wasn't a hero. He was a fraud. If he had the courage he would walk out, go home right now. But he wasn't even brave enough to do that.

Then, while all this was going through his head, his name was called. It was his turn.

CHAPTER FOURTEEN

The story was told of Columba McCann, who had saved the life of a complete stranger, Dominic Sampson, in the freezing misty waters of a loch, and of how he himself had almost died. It was a wonderful story. It didn't sound like him at all.

Ella nudged him in the ribs and whispered, 'Columba? Where did you get a name like that!'

If it had been anyone else but Ella he might have cringed with embarrassment, but Ella got his hackles up and for the first time he was proud of his name. 'Mam called both her sons after Scottish saints. That's how Mungo got his name.'

'You! Called after a saint!' Ella began to snigger but she was cut short by her mother slapping her on the hand.

'I think it's a wonderful name, Col.'

He had to be pushed to his feet when the time came. He was nervous, and felt even more that he didn't deserve to be here. He just didn't want to walk up on to that stage. He glanced at the other children gathered here. They were the real heroes, not him. He felt humble.

'Look who's giving you your award!' Ella screeched.

Col looked and saw the boy band she'd been eyeing up throughout the meal.

Nevertheless, the hall erupted in applause as Col strode to the podium, his kilt swinging proudly round him. He seemed to get an even bigger cheer because of it.

The band looked even younger when he got close to them. Not much older than Col himself.

'If there's ever anything we can do for you, Col . . .' one of them said in a soft, lilting, Irish accent as he gave him the award, a silver plaque set in midnight blue velvet.

'And don't say, *stop singing*!' one of the others yelled leading to more applause.

'Something you could do for me?' Col thought for a second. He was in such a wonderful mood, he didn't have to think for long.

He pointed towards his table. 'See that girl sitting over there, the right miserable looking one? Could you give her your autograph?'

Ella's jaw actually did fall open. Now she really looked stupid.

The lead singer held his hand over his eyes as if he was scanning the horizon. 'Ah yes, I see her . . . is that your girlfriend?'

Now, Col's jaw dropped open. He began to protest so strongly he was making the whole audience laugh.

'Is she, heck!' he yelled.

The applause and the laughter continued until he got back to his table. He expected Ella to be raging with anger for embarrassing her. But she was too delighted to be getting her own heroes' autographs.

After the awards had been presented, the real celebrations began. There was music, dancing, and cameras flashing as photographs were taken to mark the event.

Ella was in heaven as her band came and led her away, laughing and joking. Mrs Sampson, sipping champagne, edged over to Col and congratulated him again. 'Would you like to go and phone your mother?'

Col nodded. 'I'd like that.' He checked his watch. 'She's bound to be home from bingo by now.'

Mrs Sampson laughed. 'Phone from your room then.'

But Col didn't want to go back to his room. He didn't want to leave the atmosphere of this night for a second. Mrs Sampson pointed out the phone booths in the foyer and even gave him a handful of coins.

His mother was in. Lifting the phone before the second ring as if she'd been sitting there just waiting. He babbled out everything that had happened as fast as he could. Told her, too, how much he wished she was there with him.

'But it's all right, Mam,' he went on, not wanting her to feel guilty. 'I understand, and I'll have plenty of stories to tell you when I get back. And plenty of photographs. There's even gonna be a video.'

'I'll look forward to seeing that,' she said.

'Is Mungo in?' he asked. He was desperate to tell his brother about the night, hoped he, too, might have been sitting by the phone waiting for his call.

Some hope. Nothing kept his brother in.

'You'll be back tomorrow, son, and you can tell him all about it then.'

Col put the phone down, trying not to feel homesick. He was trying not to wish so hard that his mother and his brother were here with him to share the night.

And that's when he saw him. He was sure of it.

Klaus.

Somewhere by the hotel entrance, among a throng of people milling around the foyer.

Klaus?

He pushed his way forward, jumping up and down to get a clearer view.

'Klaus!' he shouted. 'Klaus!'

And there he was again. This time he saw Col too, and waited, smiling.

Col couldn't hide his surprise. 'What are you doing here?'

Klaus shrugged. 'Thought you would like someone here, just for you.'

'You came all this way . . . just for me?'

'You brought me food. You thought about me when no one else did. So I came.'

Col eyed him as if he were crazy. He thought he was crazy. And yet, he was so pleased to see him, so pleased he actually *had* come all this way for him. 'But how did you get here?'

He didn't wait for his answer. 'Did you hitch all the way here?'

Klaus nodded.

Col couldn't believe it. 'All this way, just for me?' He was truly touched.

Klaus sighed. He looked even paler than usual. In fact, he looked sick. Dark circles under his eyes, white ashen face.

He's going to die if I don't help him, Col thought. And he knew he didn't want that.

'You are my only friend, Col. You're going to help me, aren't you?'

But how could he help him? What could he do? Yet, he knew he had to do something. In a flash, he knew what that something might be.

Mr Sampson. He could help Klaus. He would know what to do. Mr Sampson was a good man. Col almost blurted it out to Klaus, but held his tongue. Time enough when they were home again. No point building up Klaus's hopes.

But Mr Sampson could help Klaus get a passport. He could help him get home. And he wouldn't have to go to prison. Maybe, Col thought, happy at the prospect, Klaus had been right. He was going to help him to get home after all.

Another good deed?

Col grinned to himself – any more of those and he'd

begin to believe he really was a superhero.

'Why do you smile?' Klaus asked him, smiling himself.

'Nothing,' Col said. 'I'm just happy.'

And he was. He felt good about himself, and about the world. 'I will help you get home, Klaus. You see if I don't. That's a promise.'

'I believe you,' Klaus said, as if it had been just what he expected of him. Suddenly, another thought occurred to Col. 'You come in and join us, Klaus. The Sampsons wouldn't mind. They're dead nice.'

Klaus looked into the warm, bustling hotel, into the warm glow of the foyer. He shook his head. 'No, Col. This is your night. And anyway, if I go in . . .' He shook his head again. 'Too many questions I can't answer.'

No amount of coaxing would convince him otherwise.

'Have you got something to eat? I could get you a carryout. There's bags of food in there.'

Klaus laughed. 'You worry about me too much. I am fine. Go. Enjoy yourself. I have to go back.'

Col thought of him on a lonely dark road, waiting, hoping for someone to give him a lift. It was a sad, miserable picture. Yet, at least he was safe from Mungo.

Mungo wouldn't find him tonight.

Col watched him go. He felt really moved that Klaus had come all this way just for him.

'Who were you speaking to?' Mrs Sampson touched his shoulder.

Col turned quickly. His face grew red. He knew he must look guilty. 'No one,' he said.

She followed his quick, furtive glance almost as if she could see Klaus. But she couldn't possibly, Col was sure of it. Klaus had already disappeared into the night, swallowed up by the crowds of London.

Col could have told her the whole story then, but he didn't. Tonight, he would forget about Klaus. Forget about everything. Just enjoy himself. Tonight was his night.

But when they were back home, then he would do everything he could to help Klaus.

CHAPTER FIFTEEN

It was pouring with rain when they landed at Glasgow airport. But nothing could dampen their high spirits – well, almost nothing.

As Mr Sampson picked up his car at the airport car park all they could talk about was their 'London Adventure', as Dominic called it. Sitting into the back seat with the boys even Miserella was laughing.

'You'll have to lose weight, Miserella,' Dominic shouted as she shoved him over with her backside. 'This is like sharing the back of the car with an elephant.'

Col let out a yell. 'That's what she reminds me of. I've been trying to figure it out for ages. I mean, the resemblance is amazing.'

For that he was elbowed hard in the ribs. But her smile remained. Nothing could wipe that smile off her face after last night. She not only had the autographs of every member of her favourite boy band, but she'd actually had her photograph taken with them, too. No, nothing could wipe that smile off her face.

Well, almost nothing.

'You know, Columba McCann, I think I could even get to like you . . . eventually . . . maybe in three or four hundred years time.'

At that, Col pretended to faint in the back seat while Dominic started to choke as if he was about to be sick.

'Suicide time!' he shouted, and started a series of jumps and kicks that made everybody yell and Ella start to slap and shake him back.

'Enough!' Mr Sampson shouted. 'I'm trying to drive here.'

But he was still smiling, too. He flicked a glance in the mirror at Col. 'I'll take this lot home, Col. Dump our luggage and then take you home. All right with you?'

'I'll get a taxi, Mr Sampson. I've got the money.'

Mrs Sampson looked shocked. 'Over my dead body. Get a taxi indeed!' She tutted. 'As if I'd allow that. In this weather. Your mother would kill me.'

It occurred to him again that Mrs Sampson was a fine woman. Thoughtful, caring, almost as good a woman as his own mother. She was loyal. Here with the Sampsons he could see a lot of loyalty. A different kind of loyalty to that of his family, but it was there just the same.

They turned into the tree-lined avenue with the windscreen wipers still struggling to clear a view of the road ahead. Mrs Sampson promised them all soup and sandwiches as soon as they went in. It was bucketing down as they hauled the cases out of the boot and struggled with them to the front door. Mr Sampson turned as he opened it. 'Well, I don't know about anyone else, but all I can say is there really is no place like home.'

Mrs Sampson stepped inside.

And screamed.

It seemed an age, as if time stopped while they took in what had happened. As they each stepped into the house.

The hall had been trashed. Graffiti was spray-painted over the walls, the furniture was scratched and daubed, the paintings were ripped. The antique unit was almost completely ruined with paint and deep gashes all over it.

And it was empty. All the china. All the silver. All the crystal. Gone.

Mrs Sampson, almost on the verge of hysteria, ran into the living room and screamed again. Carpets destroyed, furniture ruined. Everything that could be carried away easily had been taken.

'Have they done this to the whole house?' Ella sobbed.

Dominic didn't wait for an answer. He was off upstairs to check out his own room.

'But I don't understand,' Mrs Sampson cried. 'Why didn't the neighbours hear anything?'

'Because nothing they did made any noise,' Col said. 'Spray paint, slashing furniture, doesn't make a lot of noise.'

Ella's miserable face had returned, with a vengeance. 'You seem to know an awful lot about it.'

Col swallowed, feeling guilty. And something much worse, something he could hardly contemplate. He knew all this, yes, because Mungo had told him. One night when he had drunk too much and boasted of how easy it was to break into people's houses, how much fun it was to trash their homes, what a challenge it was to do it so quietly that not a soul would hear.

And Col had laughed. Not understanding that real people were involved, people like the Sampsons. People who could be hurt by such destruction of their precious things.

Ella suddenly screamed at him. 'How do you know so much!'

Mrs Sampson was still crying as she pulled her closer. 'It's not Col's fault, Ella.'

All the life seemed to have gone out of Mrs Sampson. She sank into a slashed chair and began to sob quietly.

Col felt like crying too. He blurted out, 'I'll get my brother to find out who did this. Mungo knows things. He'll find out.'

Ella laughed through her tears. 'Who are you trying to kid? Your brother did this. He knew we'd be away. The house would be empty. And you probably helped him. Was that why you decided to come to London? To get us out of the way? I hate you! I hate your whole family.'

Col ran at Mrs Sampson. 'Honest, Mrs Sampson, Mungo wouldn't do this. Not to you. Never. And I would never do a terrible thing like that. Never. But I will find out who did it. I promise.'

He was babbling, trying to understand what was happening.

And then Dominic came hurtling down the stairs

screaming. 'My PlayStation, Dad. They took my PlayStation.'

The PlayStation Dominic had taken so much pride in, had worked so hard for. Gone.

Ella ran at Col, almost pushing him off his feet. 'Don't you dare try to look as if this is hurting you!' she screamed at him. 'You don't care about us.'

Her mother pulled her back gently. She sniffed, stopped crying and stood straight. 'When it all comes down to it, it's only material things. Nobody's been hurt. We can replace material things.'

She aimed these final words at Dominic who was being comforted by his father.

Col knew then that no matter what they found out they would never blame *him*. If, because of him, their house had been broken into and trashed, they would never regret it. Because it was also because of him they still had Dominic. But knowing this didn't make him feel any better. He ached with the pain of it. As if someone had pushed a fist hard into his belly and twisted it.

In the end, he did get a taxi home. Not because Mr Sampson didn't want to take him. But because the police had arrived with a forensic team, and were asking questions about what was missing, about the professional way the house's alarm system had been disarmed, taking fingerprints with no great hope of finding any. 'A professional job' they called it.

One of the policemen took one look at Col, and that look said everything. A McCann and a burgled house, they went together like ham and eggs.

Any other time, Col would have glared at him, challenged that look. Today, he couldn't even meet his eye. He sat silently in a corner, trying to make himself invisible. Finally, he called a taxi, without telling the Sampsons until it arrived outside their door. They let him leave with only a mild protest. And as he was driven away he turned in the back seat and watched the house disappear into the grey, pouring rain.

'I'll probably never go back there,' he thought. 'I'll never be invited again. The Sampsons will never actually blame me, but they'll want to keep their distance.'

And how could he blame them for that?

He realised something else, too, He could never ask Mr Sampson to help Klaus now.

CHAPTER SIXTEEN

Mungo was sitting by the fire reading his paper when Col went in. As soon as he saw his younger brother he leapt to his feet, beaming. 'Hey, bro, missed you, pal.'

He couldn't be guilty of anything, Col reassured himself, not smiling like that, not looking so pleased to see him back. Relief flooded over him and he dropped his case and ran to him.

Mungo ruffled his hair and punched him on the chin. 'How's the hero? Got a medal?'

'Got a plaque. It's in my case.'

Mungo began heading for the kitchen. 'Mam's still working.' Col knew that already. 'But she made up sandwiches for us. Ready for some?'

'Am I ever?' Col followed Mungo. Good old Mam, he thought. She probably thought he'd be starved down in London.

Mungo made tea and small talk while Col got stuck into the sandwiches – cheese and tomato, Col's favourite. Col waited till Mungo was seated across from him at the table, hugging a mug of tea before he broached the subject of the Sampsons.

'Something terrible happened . . .' he began, dreading actually saying the words.

'What? Tell me?' Mungo looked genuinely concerned, puzzled.

It couldn't have been anything to do with Mungo, Col told himself again. He was sure of it now.

'The Sampsons' house, it was broken into, trashed, while we were away.'

Mungo chewed on a sandwich, took a sip of tea before he spoke. 'Cops got any idea who dunnit?'

Col watched him carefully. He could feel beads of cold sweat on his brow. 'I thought you might be able to help.'

Mungo tensed. 'Me?'

Col tumbled on nervously. 'You know people. You hear things. Whoever it was made an awful mess. It was just awful and the furniture was ruined, totally.'

Mungo looked unconcerned. 'Well, they've got plenty o' cash. Can afford to buy more, eh?'

He sounded callous. Col had heard him like that many times before. And before, Col would probably have laughed. But this was different. This was the Sampsons.

'They've got a really lovely place, Mungo.'

Mungo shrugged. 'Ach, they can afford to replace everything. Buy your wee pal a new PlayStation. A better one.' He laughed. 'Who cares about them anyway, Col? You're never goin' to see them again.'

Col felt his blood go cold. A shiver was running very slowly all the way down his spine. He stared at his brother. 'How did you know they took Dominic's PlayStation, Mungo?'

Mungo's neck went red. He swallowed. Col knew, then, knew beyond a doubt that it had been his brother and his mates who had broken into the Sampsons'.

'That was why you changed your mind about me going? I should have known.'

He remembered now, Mungo staring hard at Mrs Sampson and her gold. It had been envy he had seen in Mungo's gaze, nothing more. Col felt tears sting his eyes. 'I didn't want it to be you, Mungo.' His voice was cracking. 'I told them it couldn't have been you.'

Mungo slammed the table with his fist. 'You

mentioned me! You put it into somebody's napper that it *could* have been me?'

Col shouted back, just as angrily. 'I didn't have to say a word. You were the first one they suspected. I stuck up for you. I believed in you.'

'Oh, stop blubberin'! You're beginning to sound like them.'

'How could you do that? How could you steal from them? Ruin all their stuff? They're my friends, Mungo.'

''Cause it's my job!' He said it as if he was a heart surgeon, or an engineer. As if his 'job' was important, and saved lives rather than wrecked them. 'It's never bothered you before.'

No indeed. It hadn't. Col remembered the CD centre that Mungo had given him. Had another boy, just like Dominic, broken his heart when that was stolen?

It was true. Col had never cared before. But he cared now.

Mungo stood up, towering above him. Col had never seen him look so arrogant. 'You better no' tell on me.'

Col stood up, too, so quickly his chair crashed to the floor. 'How can I tell on ye, you're my brother?'

He wanted to be away from Mungo, out of this house. 'I hate you for doin' this, Mungo. Do you hear me? I hate you!'

He left the house and headed for the hills, for the loch. It was where he'd always gone when he needed to think, needed to be alone. But he didn't want to be alone now. He needed someone to talk to, someone to listen. Someone who, like him, had no one else to confide in. Klaus.

It was as if Klaus had been waiting for him, crouched by the bank, watching the swans gliding gracefully on the water. The heavy rain had become a drizzle and made the loch shimmer.

'Look at them,' Klaus nodded at the two elegant swans. 'So graceful, but you should have seen them a minute ago. Trying to land. Flapping their wings around like crazy people.' He flapped his arms to demonstrate, laughing. Then he saw that Col wasn't laughing.

'What?' he asked, concerned.

It all came tumbling out. About the break-in, the Sampsons, and Mungo's involvement.

Klaus listened, without saying a word until Col was finished. 'So, what are you going to do?'

Col looked at him. 'I can't do anything. Do you not see that? He's my brother.'

'But, Col, he betrayed you.'

And that was what hurt more than anything. Mungo had betrayed him. He had used him. Col felt like an accessory, as if he had decoyed the Sampsons to London, leaving Mungo free to do what he wanted.

And even knowing that, it didn't make any difference. 'I can't tell on him,' he said.

Klaus, for the first time since Col had known him, sounded angry. 'I don't understand you. What has he done to deserve your loyalty? Nothing. If you tell the police, the Sampsons might be able to get some of their belongings back, yet you still refuse to tell.'

'Yes!' Col snapped at him. 'You *don't* understand. Mungo doesn't have to do anything to deserve my loyalty. He's my brother. We're family. That's enough. I'll never turn on him. Never!'

Klaus's face seemed to pale in the dark of the afternoon. He took a step back from Col, almost as if he wanted to be as far away from him as possible. 'What made me ever think you could help me?' His voice sounded bitter. Not like Klaus at all.

Col had wanted to talk to Klaus, but it hadn't helped. Klaus could never understand. He turned and left him, running without a backward look. He ran back towards the lights of the town that were shimmering through the drizzle. He was angry and he was hurt.

He hated Mungo for this. What he had done had wiped out all the excitement, all the memories of his trip to London. All that seemed an age away now. It might never have happened.

And Mungo was probably right. The Sampsons would never want to see him again, and he couldn't blame them for that. It didn't matter he told himself. But deep down he knew it did. He liked the Sampsons. He even liked daft little Dominic. But he'd never see them again now.

All because of Mungo.

Yes, he hated his brother because of this.

But he'd never betray him.

CHAPTER SEVENTEEN

That night the dream came back. Rushing like a torrent through Col's troubled sleep. It was Mungo's fault. Even deep in sleep he blamed him. He hadn't had the nightmare for so long. Until now.

Only this time it was different. It was much worse.

Someone else was in the water with him, trapped under the ice, arms flailing wildly, reaching out to him, trying to pull him down deeper. Suddenly, it was Dominic – but this time he couldn't save him. They were both helpless. Then Dominic's frightened face shimmered into that of Klaus, a disappointed Klaus, wanting Col to help him, too, and knowing now he couldn't. Col tried to turn away, angry that everyone wanted his help yet there was no one to help *him*. Then, suddenly, it wasn't Klaus or Dominic whose face floated eerily in the depths. It was Mungo who was reaching out to him, but not for help.

He wanted to pull him down, down, into the murky, icy water. And for the first time in his life, Col was afraid – really afraid of his brother. He yelled himself awake as Mungo clawed towards him, almost reaching him, almost touching him, his smile becoming a skeleton's grin.

NO!

He bolted upright in his bed. He was bathed in sweat, his heart was thumping in terror. He never wanted to sleep again.

His mother had heard his yell, and burst into his room pulling on her dressing gown.

'Col, are you all right, son?' She sat on the bed beside him, holding his shoulders. 'Did you have another nightmare?'

Col nodded, wiping his brow with the edge of the sheet. He wanted so much to spill the whole story out to his mother, but it was an unwritten law that the brothers didn't involve Mam in anything Mungo got up to. She was never to be involved, never expected to provide an alibi.

Yet, she knew all about the break-in at the Sampsons, and Col was convinced she knew that Mungo was responsible. Col had been disappointed when she didn't challenge him about it, hadn't been angry with him. It was as if what Mungo did was his business and not hers.

But it was her business! She was their mother, she was supposed to be able to say anything to them.

For the first time in his life, another first, he resented his mother. She should stand up for Col. Stand up for something. In the dim light from the hallway, he looked at her as if for the first time – slim and blonde, with the black roots showing that they always teased her about. She'd never questioned Mungo's behaviour. Or Col's. They were her boys, and if they did wrong she didn't want to know about it.

And that wasn't the way it should be.

Mrs Sampson wouldn't have kept silent. Somehow, he couldn't imagine any of the Sampsons in this kind of situation, but he was sure Mrs Sampson would never allow Dominic, or Ella, to do something bad, and her not say anything about it.

His mother, unaware of these thoughts, said, 'What if I sleep in here the night? I'll wrap up in a duvet and snuggle down in the chair. Then, if you have another bad dream, I'll be right there beside you.'

Col felt a rush of guilt. A wave of love for her flowed

over him. He wanted to hug her, but they weren't a hugging kind of family. Mungo was right. He was getting more like the Sampsons.

'No, Mam, honest,' he said softly. 'I'll be fine now. You get back to bed. You've got work in the morning.'

He was sure the dream would come again after she left. He tried to force himself to stay awake. But, eventually, sleep did come. Deep, dreamless sleep.

The police came next day to interview Mungo. As they questioned him, he leaned back against the mantelpiece, master of his own house. Col watched through a crack in the door, listening to his brother throw out one well-rehearsed answer after another.

Once, it would have made him laugh watching Mungo run rings round the cops. Now, it only made him angry.

One of the policemen glanced towards the open door. 'Is that you, Col? Why don't you come and join us?'

Mungo stood erect. 'Hey, you leave my wee brother out of this.'

The policemen looked at Mungo as if he had just crawled out from under a rock. 'What are you so worried about, Mr McCann? You've got six people to alibi you. You were nowhere near the scene of the crime. We only want to say hello to Col. The Sampsons were, I believe, good to him. Fond of him even.'

He looked straight at Col now as he stepped warily into the room.

'You saw what the burglars did in that house, Col. You're probably as determined as we are to catch whoever could do that to such a nice family. Isn't that right?'

Col felt his face go red. They knew Mungo was the culprit. They knew that Col knew it, too. They were testing him.

Testing his loyalty.

But to who? Mungo, or the Sampsons?

Col shook his head. 'I wish I knew who did it.' He blurted the words out, not looking at Mungo or the police. 'But I haven't got a clue.'

'But if you did know . . . you would tell us?' the other policeman said.

Col felt Mungo's eyes burn into him, waiting for his answer.

Col was angry. Angry at them all. 'How would I ever find that out? I'm not a detective! I'm just a boy.'

He hated going back to school on Monday. News of the break-in had swept round the town. No one wanted to talk about London. It was as if it had never happened. Paul Baxter avoided him in the corridor, didn't ask for an interview, didn't ask for an article.

They all assumed he had been some kind of accessory. They all assumed his brother had been responsible.

Especially Denny. Denny thought the whole thing was exciting and dangerous. Just what he'd come to expect of the McCanns. He wanted to know all the details. It was all he wanted to talk about.

Finally, Col couldn't take any more. 'It wasn't Mungo did it, right? Get that through your thick skull, Denny. He wouldn't do that to friends of mine, or to me. And I had nothing to do with it either.'

Denny took a step back, surprised by his outburst. 'Well, that's no' what everybody's saying.'

'Well, they're wrong. And if I hear you spreading that about, I'll belt ye!'

'You'll belt me?' Now Denny looked alarmed. Alarmed and puzzled. 'You've changed, Col. I think you went into that loch as Col, and you came out as somebody else entirely.'

As Denny stalked away from him, Col shouted, 'Maybe this is the real me then.'

'I think you've changed for the better.'

He turned at the unmistakably husky voice of Blaikie. Her hair was even blacker than usual, standing out in spikes round her head, like a chargrilled Statue of Liberty.

'What do you mean? I've changed for the better?'

Blaikie shrugged, blew a fat, slow bubble. Sucked it back into her mouth before she answered. 'You're easier to talk to. Nicer. Everybody says it. Not just me.' She chewed thoughtfully. 'Even Mrs Holden's getting to like you.'

That was true, and it was strange that Blaikie, of all people, should have noticed that. He smiled at her.

She smiled back. Her face was so white, her teeth looked yellow. 'See,' she said. 'You've never smiled at me in your life.'

'I wish you'd wash that muck off your face, Blaikie. You'd be a real cracker if you didn't wear that make-up.'

For a minute he was sure she was going to spit her chewing gum at him, but then, she smiled again. 'If you say Mungo didn't do it, I'll believe you.'

In that second, Col realised he wanted to tell her everything. He needed somebody to confide in, maybe Blaikie was the one. She would listen. She would understand.

But the moment passed as Col heard a familiar, excited voice calling him from across the playground.

'Col! Col!'

It was Dominic, jumping about at the school gates, and with him, looking grim, was Mr Sampson.

CHAPTER EIGHTEEN

Dominic came running up to him, and began pulling on his hand. 'Come on, Col.'

Col was sweating as he was dragged towards the school gates.

'You're for it now,' Denny sneered at him as he passed. Denny, once his best pal, was now wishing more trouble on him. Mr Sampson wasn't even looking Col's way. He kept his back to him, studying the road intently.

Col saw his headmaster emerge from the school building. He caught sight of Mr Sampson. Col saw recognition on his face. Then alarm as he saw Col heading towards him. Col had seen that look many times before. Waiting for trouble. Expecting it from the McCanns.

Col could hardly listen to Dominic's chattering. Only

caught snatches of it.

'My dad's got the car. Wants you to go with him.'

Col's heart was bursting through his chest. Wants me to go with him? he thought. Where?

To the police station probably.

Out of the corner of his eye he could see his headmaster watching closely, waiting. And not just *his* eyes, the eyes of all the other pupils in the playground.

Mr Sampson turned as Col approached. Col stopped dead. He was aware of all the eyes of the school turned towards him, from the playground, from teachers, from windows. Everyone.

And, suddenly, to his surprise, Mr Sampson smiled. 'Hello, Col. How are you?'

Col couldn't answer. His mouth was dry. He was too surprised. He glanced quickly back into the playground. The tension there seemed to have dropped. The headmaster was still heading for his car, still darting quick glances towards the school gates. But he seemed more relaxed now.

Col looked back at Mr Sampson. 'Why did you come here?' he asked, puzzled.

Dominic answered, bouncing with enthusiasm as usual. 'We're all going out for a meal. It's my mum's birthday. You're coming too. We've already phoned your mum. It's OK.'

He stopped for breath and Mr Sampson smiled again. 'He manages to tell a whole story in ten seconds.'

Col still couldn't believe it. 'You want *me* to go with you?'

Mr Sampson nodded. 'If you'd like to. We'd like you to be there.'

They could have phoned to ask him. Picked him up at the house, or he could have met them at the restaurant. There were plenty of alternatives to actually coming to the school to ask him.

'Why did you come . . . *here*?' Col asked again.

But he knew why, even before Mr Sampson answered. 'Because we don't want anybody, here at school – anywhere – thinking we blame you. We don't, Col.'

Dominic pulled at his sleeve. 'You're going to come, right? 'Cause I'm not going if you don't come.'

It wasn't going to be easy, spending time with the Sampsons, knowing what Mungo had done. But if they could suffer him, he would do it. It was the least he could do.

'I'd like to come,' Col said softly. 'If you're sure.'

Dominic had no doubts. 'Of course we're sure.'

141

'We'll pick you up then,' Mr Sampson said. 'About seven?'

'No!' Col said it too quickly. But he couldn't have the Sampsons sitting in the car outside his house, and Mungo inside. Col in the middle of it all. No. He took a deep breath. 'I'll meet you at the restaurant, if that's OK.'

Mr Sampson didn't object. So it was decided, and Col wasn't sure if he was doing the right thing or not.

It had begun to rain by the time he got home, and the rain became a storm as the afternoon darkened.

He had thought Mam would have objected to his going. She might pretend she didn't suspect Mungo, but Col knew she was just as aware as he was of Mungo's guilt.

Of course he soon found out why. Mungo hadn't been in all day. He didn't know a thing about it.

'And there's no need to tell him where you've been,' she said, as she stood ironing Col's shirt.

'I did try to say no, Mam,' he said.

She smiled. 'I know, son. It's awful hard to say no to that wee Dominic.'

Col took a bus into town, but even on the short dash to the restaurant, he was soaked by the time he got there.

Dominic was waiting for him in the doorway. 'We should have picked you up.' He dragged him in out of the rain. 'We've got a great table. Come on.'

This was the part he'd been dreading. Walking towards that table to face Mrs Sampson. Yet already she was standing, moving forward to greet him. Already she was smiling.

How could she do that?

She must know Mungo was the main suspect. The police would have told her that.

The answer was tugging at Col's sleeve. Dominic.

'Come and sit by me, Col,' she said. 'Take off that wet jacket.'

She called a waiter over and asked him to hang the jacket somewhere so it would dry.

'How are you, Mrs Sampson?'

She didn't get a chance to answer Col's question. Ella did that. 'Oh, she's just wonderful. Half her furniture's destroyed, and the other half's been stolen. She's just wonderful.' Then she sneered at him. 'Moron!'

'Ella!' her mother warned. 'Be quiet!'

Ella wanted to say more. Spit out all the venom she'd been building up since the burglary, but her mother wouldn't let her.

'This is my birthday. I want to forget for a while. Have a nice meal. Just enjoy ourselves.'

It was the hardest two hours of Col's life. They couldn't talk about London. (London, a million years away now.) It reminded everyone of what they'd come home to.

I shouldn't have come, Col thought, again and again. Yet, if they were willing to sit through this, how could he have refused? They wanted to show the world they trusted him.

If he could force Mungo to give everything back, he would. But even giving everything back wouldn't make a difference. Too much had been destroyed.

Ella got her chance to confront him when her mother went off to the ladies room and Mr Sampson was paying the bill. 'I don't know how you had the nerve to come here, Col McCann. After what you did.'

'Col didn't do anything,' Dominic almost shouted. 'I'm going to tell Dad you said that!'

'Shut up!' Ella said it so fiercely, Dominic did just that. 'I won't get a chance to talk to you again. I hope I never set eyes on you, but I just want you to know how much I hate you. Why can't you admit it was your brother? How could he do those things? We've only ever been nice to you – and your horrible family.'

144

'It wasn't Mungo—' Col didn't sound convincing, even to himself.

'You know it was him. Just admit that. That's all I'm asking, and maybe then I wouldn't hate you so much.'

She glared at him, her teeth clenched tight. 'Just say it!' There were tears in her eyes. Tears of anger.

Col couldn't hold that tearful, angry gaze. 'It wasn't him,' was all he could say.

She pushed her chair back, threw her napkin on the table and stormed off.

'She doesn't like you, Col,' Dominic said it so innocently that Col almost smiled. 'But she's the only one. My mum and dad think you're brilliant. And you're still my hero.'

He wasn't anybody's hero, Col thought bitterly. Maybe he never had been.

Mr Sampson got him a taxi home, and as he watched them through the driving rain he wondered if this really was the last time he would see them.

The storm was growing worse by the minute. Rain bounced off the pavements, and every few minutes the sky was lit up by the lightning. The wildest storm he had seen in a long time.

But there was even more of a storm waiting for him when he got home.

CHAPTER NINETEEN

Mungo stood in front of the roaring fire, his hands on his hips, legs apart, looking fierce. He reminded Col of a photo of the Colossus of Rhodes he'd once seen in a school text book.

Col stood at the living-room door, staring right back at his brother. It was clear that somehow he had found out where Col had been.

It was Mungo who broke the silence. 'Did you tell them anythin'?'

'You mean like, "My brother had a great time at your place the other night. He really hopes you liked his redecorations."?'

Mungo took a threatening step towards him and Col stepped back.

For the first time, apart from in his dream, he was afraid of his brother. Afraid he'd . . . what? Did he really believe Mungo would hurt him?

'You never should have went with them!'

'Do you know what they asked me for? To show people they trusted me. They know you did it – everybody knows you did it – but they wanted to show they still trusted *me*! They're nice people, Mungo. And you . . . you should never have done what you did!'

Mungo's voice was a sneer. 'They're nice people . . . wi' money!'

'They work hard for it,' Col snapped back.

'Ach well, they can work harder then.'

Col realised he could never make Mungo understand. 'What would you know about work? You've never worked in your life.'

Mungo's eyes flashed with rage. 'Don't you dare talk to me like that. You better show me some respect.'

'Respect for you!' Col was every bit as angry. 'What respect did you show me? Look at the position you've put me in!'

'What position?' Mungo threw the words at him. 'You're my brother. You don't tell on a brother. End of story. You stick to that and you've not got a problem.'

In that second Col hated his brother, and all he stood for. Mostly because he knew he was right. He could never betray him. 'Don't worry yourself. I'm never going to see them again anyway.' And he knew this time it was true. He'd known it since Mrs Sampson had hugged him so tightly outside the restaurant. She was saying *goodbye*.

Mungo relaxed. 'Good. That's what I wanted to hear.' He said it as if he'd won, as if Col had done exactly what he wanted.

'I hate you, Mungo!' Col yelled at him.

But Mungo only laughed and called after him as he pounded upstairs to his room. 'You'll feel better in the mornin', bruv.'

He thought he would never sleep. His mind was too full of the Sampsons, and Mungo. He'd never felt such misery in all his life.

Even when he did drop into a troubled doze another crack of thunder would awaken him with a start. The room would light up and the rain seemed to be battering its way through the windows.

He did finally sleep. But it brought him no rest.

Dreams.

Dreams of rain and thunder and ice.

Once again, he was trapped in that dark icy loch, going under, the waters closing round him like a shroud. He tried to call out but no sound came and water filled his mouth and made him choke. He could see the ice above him closing over his head. He tried to reach up, break through, but it was too far. Dominic's face appeared, dim and hazy, calling to him. And Mrs Sampson, reaching down, wanting to help, to drag him to safety but the ice was between them.

And then, from nowhere, Mungo appeared, towering over them, a nightmare grin on his face. Col tried to shout to them, to warn them, but no sound came. Deeper and deeper he swirled into the silent depths of the loch. Reeds tangled round his ankles, like snakes dragging him down. The faces above him were growing ever more distant, and long icy ferns touched his face. He wanted to live so much.

He thrashed and turned and saw dark eerie shapes coming towards him through the dark water. He tried to turn away, didn't want to see what he dreaded. He wanted to wake up.

Then, in the silent depths he felt something behind him, something he'd shut out so many times before. Closer it came, touching his shoulder, edging him round. He didn't want to look. He wanted to surge to the surface, but he was held in a nightmare trance.

He turned, he couldn't stop himself. And there, rising in the water before him, a face . . . a body . . .

A body.

Col screamed himself awake as yet another crack of thunder rent the air.

A body!

It wasn't a nightmare. It was a memory. A memory he had been pushing away from him all this time. Waking up always before he had to confront it.

It hadn't been the face of Death he had seen so long ago in the water. It had been a human face.

There had been a body in the loch.

He had glimpsed it that day, so close he could have reached out and touched it. The terror of that vision was what had sent him hurtling to the surface.

He jumped out of his bed. His pyjamas clung to his body with sweat. He had to tell Mungo. Mungo would know what to do.

Mungo was sitting by the fire, watching the late night boxing on TV. He turned as Col stumbled into the room, sat up when he saw his ashen face. 'What's wrong?'

Col's voice trembled. 'I was dreaming. A nightmare. But it was worse this time, Mungo. And it wasn't a nightmare. It was real. Mungo . . . that day in the loch.'

He let out a sob. 'There was a body down there. I saw it. It . . . touched me, Mungo.' He ran to his brother, clutched at his shirt. 'Mungo, it must still be there.'

Mungo's eyes were ice cold. He plucked Col's fingers from him. He shook his head. 'Why the hell did you have to go to that loch in the first place!'

'What does that matter? There's a body down there.'

Mungo let out a long, slow sigh. He looked at Col for what seemed an age. 'Who do you think put it there?' he said at last.

Col gasped. He stepped back. His brother, capable of anything, but not this.

'Do you mean you . . .?' Col couldn't say the words.

'There was a chase. There was a fight. I won. OK? Now, he's down there and he's stayin' down there. Right? Just forget your dream.'

Col was shaking now. 'I can't believe you'd do anything like that.'

Suddenly, Mungo had him by the shoulders. 'Grow up, Col. You've got to keep your mouth shut about this. For my sake . . . and for yours.' He grinned. 'You being an accomplice an' all.'

Col couldn't take that in. Didn't understand it. He was still trapped in the nightmare. He must be. 'Me? An accomplice?'

The sky lit up again and Mungo pointed outside. 'A night like this. Remember? There was a belter of a storm, I came running in, the cops after me. You and me rollin' about in the garden, pretendin' we were fightin'. Remember now? You gave me my alibi. You're in this as deep as me, son.'

Mungo spoke as if he hated him. Col had never heard his brother talk to him like that before. Col saw his life stretching ahead of him, always in Mungo's power, always doing what Mungo wanted. He shook his head.

'No!'

Mungo threw Col from him. 'What's the point of telling anybody? The guy's dead. Has anybody missed him? No. And do you know why? He was a nobody. A nothing. He deserved everything he got. He's better off dead. He was only a dirty illegal immigrant, shacking up in one of them old air-raid shelters at the loch.'

Col felt as if the air had been punched out of him. Black spots appeared in front of his eyes. He grabbed the back of a chair, sure he was about to faint.

An illegal immigrant? But Klaus had said *he* was the only illegal immigrant at the loch . . .

CHAPTER TWENTY

No. It couldn't be Klaus he was talking about. And yet . . .
suddenly, it was the face of Klaus he could imagine
drifting at him through the water.

No!

Mungo grabbed for him as he staggered, but Col
pulled away from him. 'You killed him,' he muttered.
His mind racing, trying to sort things clear in his head.

That was how Klaus had known so much about
Mungo. Hated him so much. He shook the unnerving
thought away. Can't be . . . couldn't be possible. If that
was true, it would mean Klaus was dead. Klaus had
always been dead. That Klaus was a—

No!

But Mungo *had* killed someone.

'What's wrong wi' ye, boy?' Mungo's voice was harsh.

Col kept backing away from him, his mind in turmoil.

Trying desperately to think.

No one else had seen Klaus. No one but him. Not at the hospital. Not at the loch. Not in London.

'You get back to your bed! Forget what I've told you. Or else!'

He had to get away from Mungo. Col was at the front door. He grabbed for his jacket, still damp from earlier.

'Where do you think you're goin'?'

Col didn't answer. He hauled open the door. The storm crashed its way through. And he ran. Ran into the night.

The wall of rain pounded against his face so hard he could hardly keep his eyes open. Hardly see where he was going. But he didn't need to see. His feet were leading him up through the estate, over the hill, and to the loch.

He would find Klaus there. Taking shelter from the storm. Not a ghost.

He would explain everything. It had been another illegal immigrant. Had to be.

He had taken food to Klaus, and the duvet. Ghosts don't eat. They don't feel cold. Do they?

Yet, even as he ran, he remembered. He had never seen Klaus actually eat anything. Klaus had never told him he was cold, or hungry. And Col had put so many words into Klaus's mouth. Explaining to himself how he had come to London. Had he already suspected there was something strange about Klaus? Had he always felt there was something he was holding back from telling him?

There was only one thing Klaus had ever wanted from Col. He had only ever asked one thing of him. Help me get back home. Growing paler and weaker with every meeting, fading from him. As if he had only a limit of time to ask for Col's help. And he so wanted Col to help him, but he knew too well that the only way he could do that would be to betray his brother.

And what good would that do? What's done is done. Mungo was right.

But Klaus was alive. He had to be. There are no such things as—

He was afraid as he neared the pitch black loch. The trees were eerie, waving, silhouettes against the sky. Afraid of what he might find here.

For the first time, afraid of Klaus.

Col stood for a moment at the lochside. He was wet through, shivering with fear and cold, straining his eyes to see.

Suddenly, another flash of lightning illumined the whole landscape – and Col gasped.

There was Klaus, standing only a few feet away from him, watching him, waiting for him. Paler than ever, almost transparent.

Col knew his worst nightmare was true. There was no other illegal immigrant. The body weighted down in the water was Klaus. He had been dead since the first time they'd met. Unimaginable as it was, it was true.

'I've been waiting for you, Col. I knew you'd come.' Even Klaus's voice seemed to drift, ghost-like in the wind.

Col wanted to cry, his voice was a sob. 'I don't believe this. I don't understand.'

'Believe it, Col,' Klaus's voice was so soft, yet Col heard it perfectly above the storm. 'I don't understand either. But I'm here. A force more powerful than death has held me here so that you can help me. Tell them who I am. Tell them to send me home to my family.'

And now he knew why, that night in the shelter, Klaus had told him so much about his village, about his family. He was leading up to this moment.

Col screamed. 'I can't tell them about you! They'd find out it was my brother who did this. What does it matter now?'

'It matters to me, Col. Help me. I want to go home to my mother and my sisters.' Now, Klaus was crying softly. So sad, so lonely. 'I don't want to lie in the dark waters of the loch for ever.'

'I can't do it, Klaus. Don't ask me. Please, don't ask me.'

'I can't hold on much longer.' Col could see how true that was. Death, cheated for so long, was pulling him closer. 'You are my only hope. Help me, Col. Help me.'

'NO!'

Col stumbled back, began to run, away from the loch. He took one last backward look at Klaus, hardly visible, hardly there, still calling after him.

'Help me . . .'

Col ran on, splashing through puddles, flooded gutters, through rivers gushing down the streets. His mind caught in as much of a storm as his body.

To help Klaus would be the end of Mungo. He'd be arrested, jailed. Mungo, who hated to be shut up. He couldn't do that to his own brother. It was against everything he believed in.

Yet, how could they prove it was Mungo who had killed Klaus? They couldn't. Could they?

But what if they did?

It was too much of a risk to take.

He had run without thinking and here he was on the street where the Sampsons lived. He hadn't realised he had been heading this way, but he knew why he was here.

He trusted them. They'd know what to do.

He banged madly on their door, oblivious to the storm. A light came on upstairs. Col shouted, 'Mr Sampson. It's me, Col. Please let me in.'

A moment later light flooded the hall and the front door was hauled open.

'Col! What have you been doing?' Mr Sampson pulled Col out of the driving rain and into the warm welcoming house. Even in the storm, there was a warmth that enveloped this house.

Mrs Sampson was there too, trying to get Col's wet jacket off, but he struggled against her.

How could he explain this to them? What could he say? They'd never believe him. He still hardly believed it himself. 'I don't know what to do,' was all he could manage to say.

'Come to the fire. Tell us about it.'

But he couldn't move, shivering and dripping on to

the scratched and defaced wood of their floor.

'I'll believe you,' Mrs Sampson said, and Col thought that of all of them she was the one who probably would. She had sensed Klaus at the hospital, thought she saw him at the hotel.

He clutched at her hand. 'I'm so mixed up. I don't want to hurt anybody. I don't know what's the right thing to do.'

She touched his face. 'You'll always do the right thing, Col.'

'Tell me about it, Col. Let me help.' Mr Sampson's voice was full of concern.

Maybe, Col thought in a flash of inspiration as bright as the lightning, he could tell Mr Sampson about the body in the loch. Tell him he had thought it was a dream. But it wasn't. It was a locked up memory that had been too horrible to face. Things like that happened, didn't they? Mr Sampson would know how to explain it – Col wouldn't be involved then, Mungo couldn't blame him, and Klaus would go home.

In the next instant he realised he couldn't involve the Sampsons. Mungo would take his revenge on them, would feel he had a right to.

No. Col couldn't involve anyone else.

It was then that Dominic appeared on the stairs, rubbing sleep from his eyes.

'You all right, Col?'

Col looked up at him, and in Dominic's eyes all he could see was admiration. To him, Col was the best person who had ever lived, the big brother he didn't have.

'Dominic,' he asked, 'would you ever betray me?'

Dominic's eyes went wide with horror. 'Never, Col. Never.'

'No matter what I did?'

No hesitation from Dominic. 'I'd die before I'd turn against you. No matter what you did.'

Col was reminded of another stormy night – so long ago – when he had said the same thing to his brother. 'I'd die before I'd turn against you.'

And he realised he didn't want Dominic to be the same as he was. He didn't ever want him to face this kind of dilemma. He wanted him to be his own person. Do the right thing. Always.

He pulled away from the Sampsons. 'It's OK,' he muttered, 'I'm all right now.'

He ran through the doorway and out into the night. The Sampsons shouted after him, but he didn't stop. He knew what he had to do now.

CHAPTER TWENTY-ONE

He almost collapsed with exhaustion when he burst through his front door an hour later.

His mother, frantic with worry, ran to him in tears. 'Col, what have you been doing, for heaven's sake?' She hauled him to his feet. 'You're shivering. You've probably caught double pneumonia. Oh son! Come to the fire.' She glared into the living room where Mungo stood watching Col closely, his face stern.

'That Mrs Samspon phoned. Said you'd been there. In a state, she said.' Mungo's voice was barely holding in his fury.

'She was that worried about you.' His mother was leading him gently towards the fire. 'What's wrong, son? What's happened?'

She caught the look that passed between the brothers. 'Has something happened wi' you two?' Her eyes settled on Mungo. 'What have you done now?'

Even Col was surprised at her tone. He'd seldom heard his mother talk like that to Mungo. Accusing him.

Mungo snapped at her. 'Me? Ask him what he's done!'

'In the mornin'. In the mornin'.' Mam was on the edge of tears. 'I can't handle this now.'

She settled Col in a chair by the roaring fire. 'I'm going to run a bath for you. Get you out of those wet clothes.' She took a step back and looked at him, and the realisation that he'd been running through the storm in his pyjamas and slippers hit her again. 'Why, son? Why?'

She didn't wait for his answer. She didn't want to hear it. She was too aware it had something to do with Mungo. As she left the brothers alone the dark look she shot at her elder son warned him not to make more trouble. Col shivering in the chair. Mungo standing over him. Col couldn't stop shaking. The cold, the rain, the shock, had all seeped into his bones.

'Right. You've been to the Sampsons. Probably told them everything. Where else have you been, ya wee grass? The cops? You told the cops?'

Col looked up at him. How could he ever tell him what he had just done? Why couldn't he talk to him the way he used to? Or, had he ever really talked to Mungo? Had he only ever listened – in awe at his exploits? Never questioning, never going against him – until now.

Col's voice wavered when finally he did speak. 'I didn't tell the Sampsons anything. I promise.'

Mungo looked as if he wasn't sure whether to believe him or not.

'And the cops?'

Col's hesitation told him all he needed to know. 'You grassed me up! My brother grassed me up!' He looked as if he was ready to take a swipe at him.

Col shook his head. 'No, I didn't. Nobody could connect you or me with that body. Honest, Mungo . . . I just made a phone call. An anonymous phone call.'

He saw himself back in the vandalised call box. Dialling 999, telling a snotty-voiced woman there was a body in the loch, deep in the loch, telling her exactly where to find it. Telling her all about Klaus. What his name was, where he came from. Remembering every detail that Klaus had told him that cold night in the air-raid shelter.

Finally, telling her to send him home.

He had refused to answer any of her questions.

'How do you know about this body?'

'What is your name?'

None of that mattered, his quivering voice told her. Just get the body out. He wants to go home.

Then he'd hung up.

No mention of Mungo. No way surely of tying his brother to the body in the loch. No way of connecting Col to the phone call.

Klaus would be found. He would be lifted from the dark waters he was so afraid of. He would be sent home to his mother and his sisters. Buried in his homeland.

It was the best he could do for Klaus, and it was the most difficult decision he ever had to take.

He shook himself back from the memory. 'You won't be connected to it, Mungo.' He assured him. 'But I just couldn't leave him down there.'

Suddenly, Mungo lifted him by the shoulders. 'Him? You talk as if you know him personally.'

Mungo's eyes were exactly the same colour as Col's, but there was an ice in them that Col hoped he didn't have. How could he possibly tell him? It was too unbelievable.

'I know how scared I was in that water, Mungo. I just wanted out. How could I let anybody else rot in there for ever? I couldn't do it. Not even for you.'

And that, at least, was true. He could never have let Klaus stay down there, lost, alone, unknown, for eternity.

'You leave Col be!' Mam bounded back into the room. Col had never heard her so angry. Never heard her so angry at Mungo.

Mungo sprang back, released Col. It had taken him aback too. 'You don't know what he's done, Mam.'

Suddenly, she sprang at Mungo. 'I know he's your brother.'

Mungo's eyes flashed with anger. 'He's no brother of mine!'

Mam screamed. 'He's a better brother than you deserve. I've let you off with too much, Mungo. Just like I let your daddy off. But not any more. I want Col to have a better life. He could have a better life. And I won't let you ruin it for him.'

She was yelling at the top of her voice so frantically and with such anger that Col started shaking again. But Mungo was angry too. Suddenly, he lifted his hand and—

'That's right! Hit me! Just try it!'

Mungo stepped back. Afraid of his own fury. Afraid, too, of his own mother's anger.

Mam wrapped the warm blanket around Col's shoulders. 'Come on, son,' she said softly. She didn't look at Mungo. 'You should never have done what you did to that nice family, Mungo.' She led Col upstairs, and didn't answer, didn't listen as Mungo tried to protest, tried to put all the blame on Col.

She thinks it has something to do with the burglary, Col thought. His mother could never imagine that her son, bad as he was, could ever do anything as evil as murder.

But it would be all right now. Col was sure of it.

It had to be.

CHAPTER TWENTY-TWO

Over the next few days the papers were full of the story. The body dragged from the loch. The mysterious, anonymous phone call that led the police to the grim discovery. There were pleas for the caller to come forward, but no mention, no connection to Col, or Mungo, or the McCanns. Col heard it all through a haze, wrapped safely in a cocoon of fever brought on by his night in the storm.

The police didn't come to the house when they found the body, and Col rested easier after that. No one came for Mungo, and with Klaus identified, he would soon be at rest in his own land. Mungo was safe.

The police still didn't come.

Col was off school all that week. He and Mungo were barely speaking.

Almost the whole week had passed before the police came.

Four of them. Two in uniform. Two in plain clothes.

Col sat in the kitchen while they questioned his brother in the living room. His heart was thumping wildly inside him.

'What's this got to do wi' me?' he heard Mungo snarl. 'You've got nothing on me!'

The policeman's voice was calm. 'We'd like you to accompany us to the police station, Mr McCann.'

Suddenly, Mungo's voice was shrill and loud. 'Mam! Phone my lawyer!'

Mam was in the kitchen with Col, apparently intent on shredding cabbage. She closed her eyes and took a deep breath, then wiping her hands on her apron she hurried into the living room. 'I will, son.'

Col got up too, and stood at the kitchen door and watched as Mungo was led from the house. He wanted to run to him, to let him know how much he still loved him, but he was too afraid to move. Mungo turned as he passed him, his eyes ablaze with anger. 'Satisfied noo, wee man?' And before Col could say a word Mungo spat in his face. Col reeled back, shocked.

'I don't know why you're mad at your brother, Mr McCann,' one of the uniformed policemen said. 'It's your mates you should be angry with.'

Now Mungo turned on him. 'What?'

The policeman couldn't help but look smug. 'Seems your mates don't have any loyalty at all. First chance they got they spilled their guts out, making sure you got most of the blame. They're not going to carry the can for this one.'

Mungo almost leapt at him, but the other policeman held him back.

'You're trying to trick me.' But there was no real conviction in his voice. Mungo was uncertain now. Couldn't be sure just how much the police knew. He was dragged out of the house, shouting abuse at the police, swearing vengeance at all who had wronged him, including his brother.

'I'm sorry, Mam,' Col said, when Mungo had gone. His voice was shaking.

'It's not your fault, Col,' she said. And then, suddenly, her face crumpled and his Mam began to cry. 'I knew he was a bad lad, but not this . . . not murder. Not my son.' She seemed to sag inside her clothes, and Col gently held her and sat with her on the stairs.

'I'm the one to blame,' she cried quietly. 'Letting him off with so much. I knew what he was doing, but I kept thinking . . . he'll change. He'll grow out of it. But he had bad blood in him. Your dad's bad blood. I thought if I gave you both a happy home, and love, Mungo wouldn't turn out the same as his dad.' She looked at Col through her tear-filled eyes. 'Your dad had such a horrible upbringing, that's what made him bad. I tried to change that for him, because I knew he was good, deep down. I thought I could change Mungo too.'

'Don't cry, Mam.' Col couldn't bear that. He still felt it was all his fault. No matter what she said. He put his arm round her waist. 'Mungo's got good in him. We know that.'

She looked at him as if she could never believe that now. 'You're different, Col. You've always been different. There's so much good in you. So much thoughtfulness. I know you always thought Mungo was my favourite, but he never was. You have to believe that, son. You were that easy to love. But Mungo, he was hard work. I thought if I was there all the time, I could keep him out of trouble, real trouble. I thought I could influence him. You don't know how much I wanted to go to London with you. But I was frightened to go away and leave your brother.' She sobbed again. 'And look what he did when you were in London, eh? Some good I was!' She hugged Col even closer. 'Mungo was your age when your dad got killed. Your dad was his hero. He wanted to be just like him. I thought I could turn him from that . . . but it was too late for your dad, and it's too late for Mungo. Too late.'

Col's mother had never spoken to him like this. Never said a bad word against Mungo. Family loyalty. She believed in it so much.

What would she do if she knew that he had betrayed that loyalty?

She held her apron to her face and cried bitterly against it. Col hated to see her cry like this. Didn't know what to say to make her feel better.

'It's not too late, Mam. You'll see. We'll both help Mungo.'

He didn't know how long they sat there, holding each other. A long time. But, finally, his mam stopped crying and stood up. She wiped away the tears with the palms of her hands. 'Come on, Col. Help me make the tea. We'll be fine. You and me. And as for Mungo. He'll be back. Mungo always comes back.'

But this time he didn't. Charged and held without bail Mungo didn't come back to the house at all. In the end it wasn't just his friends who had turned on him. Mungo had pointed the guilty finger at himself. There was enough of his skin tissue under the corpse's nails to put Mungo's guilt beyond any reasonable doubt.

Col had plenty of visitors though.

Blaikie came to see him, knocking timidly at the front door.

Timidly? Blaikie? Never. But she did, and she looked nervous as Col's mam led her in. His mother raised an inquisitive eyebrow at the visitor. She was dying to ask who this girl was who had come to visit her son. It was the brightest Col had seen her since Mungo's arrest. Col introduced her, and Mam left them alone. 'I'll be in the kitchen baking scones.'

'I'd love to be able to bake scones,' Blaikie said with an enthusiasm Col had never heard before.

His mother responded with just as much enthusiasm. 'Come in with me, then, when you're ready. We'll make them together.'

Mam didn't tell her she was making the scones for the Sampsons. Mrs Sampson had phoned that morning to ask if it would be possible to visit Col. His mam had agreed reluctantly. It could be a difficult visit. Everyone knew, though it would probably never be proved, that Mungo was responsible for the burglary at the

Sampsons' house, and Col knew his mother would find it hard to face them.

But as the day passed she had become increasingly more enthusiastic. 'They're such a nice family, Col. A good family. And they think the world of you.'

And so, the scones.

When the Sampsons arrived ten minutes after Blaikie, Col answered the door. Only Mr Sampson was missing, working late. Even Ella was there, striding into the hall looking all around her.

'Approve, do you, madam?' Col asked.

Ella smirked. 'Just checking if any of our stuff's still here.'

Dominic jumped at her. 'You leave Col be. You promised.'

Col pulled Dominic back. 'Oh, come on, Dominic. The lassie was born to moan. Let her enjoy it.'

Mam hurried from the kitchen to greet them. 'Mrs Sampson. Dominic.' She beamed at him. She liked Dominic. Everyone did. 'How are you, son?'

Mrs Sampson hugged her, taking his mother totally by surprise. 'I'm so sorry, Mrs McCann, about . . . Mungo. I know how you must be feeling.'

His mother was red-faced with embarrassment when

she escaped from that hug, but she appreciated the gesture. 'It's that nice of you to come,' she said. 'I'm glad. For Col's sake.'

Blaikie appeared at the kitchen door, glaring at Ella. She seemed to be back to her usual threatening face. A face that was even whiter than usual, but this time with flour. 'We're making scones,' she said to no one in particular, but it was Ella who answered. 'You make them, and I'll eat them.'

Blaikie looked as if she was ready to throttle Ella, but Col and Dominic only laughed.

'I think they both fancy you, Col,' Dominic said, and Ella's mouth went as round as a hula-hoop with shock.

'I would have to have no brain and be totally desperate,' Ella snapped.

Dominic grinned. 'You pass on both counts, sister.' He looked at Col. 'Which one do *you* fancy, Col?'

Dominic ended up in the kitchen, too, helping his mother and Blaikie to make the scones. Ella went in too, though she insisted she had no interest in making scones.

'I was meant for greater things,' she said haughtily. And was annoyed when everyone just laughed.

Mrs Sampson sat with Col. 'Everything sorted out now, Col?' she asked.

'I don't know yet,' he said. 'Mungo won't talk to me. Says he'll never talk to me again.' Col didn't explain why. Somehow, he felt he didn't need to. 'And my Mam's in the middle and it's really hard for her. She's got the court case to go through and her two sons aren't talking. Mungo doesn't even want me to visit.'

'Maybe time will help Mungo understand. He's your brother. In spite of everything I bet he still loves you.'

Col wanted so much for that to be true. Wanted so much for Mungo to change, to understand. 'I'm sorry about that night I came to your house. I was mixed up. I didn't know what to do.'

She touched his hand gently. 'I understand, Col.'

Something in her did understand, about Klaus, about Mungo, about Col. He didn't know why, or how, but he just knew she did.

Suddenly, Dominic came rushing into the living room covered in flour. 'Mum, I know exactly what I want to be when I grow up. I want to be a baker!'

Mrs Sampson looked at Col and smiled.

'Wow!' Col laughed. 'I've saved the life of a future baker.'

He went back to the loch just once more – with Dominic.

He didn't know what he expected to find. But there was nothing. No mysterious presences, no Klaus, no strange atmosphere.

Only a calmness on the water. Peace.

The breeze shimmered through the trees and the swans and their tiny cygnets left a glittering trail on the surface of the loch.

'I love coming here, Col,' Dominic said. 'It's special, isn't it?' He skimmed a stone across the surface. 'You would never think a body had been down there all that time, eh?'

Col said nothing, but he thought of his friend, Klaus, and his pale, sad face.

'Still,' Dominic went on, skimming another stone. 'That guy's home now. I think that would make him happy, eh, Col?'

Col skimmed a stone too, rippling across the calm waters. A family of ducks followed in the wake of the swans and their cygnets. New life.

Klaus was home now, with his mother and his sisters.

Col had kept his promise.